Another chance?

"Megan is the only person I've ever met who is both a couch potato *and* a certified airhead," Big Guy continued. "I've learned you can only spend a finite amount of time just looking at someone before you go out of your mind with boredom." He rolled his eyes.

I hardened my heart. "Look, why did you come here? Why are you telling me this? Are you looking for advice? Approval? Do I look like Ann Landers?"

He reached across the table and grabbed my hand. I tried to pull away. "I came to say how sorry I am that what happened happened. And that I'm sorry for the way I handled it. But most of all that I want you to give me another chance."

Other Apple Paperbacks you will enjoy:

I Thought You Were My Best Friend
by Ann Reit

Twin Switch
by Carol Stanley

You, Me, and Gracie Makes Three
by Dean Marney

The Secret Diary of Katie Dinkerhoff
by Lila Perl

BIG GUY,
Little Women

Jacqueline Shannon

AN
APPLE
PAPERBACK

SCHOLASTIC INC.
New York Toronto London Auckland Sydney

ISBN 0-590-41685-5

12 11 10 9 8 7 6 5 4 3 2 1   9/8 0 1 2 3 4/9

Printed in the U.S.A.   01
First Scholastic printing, June 1989

For J.D. and Mary Ann Trobaugh,
with love and thanks

First Scholastic printing, June 1986

Chapter 1

Lori Laigen leads a lucky life.

I found those words scrawled across my locker in thick, red felt pen after my last class on that ominously important January day last year, the day it all started.

"Who wrote that?" I wondered aloud.

"You did," said my best friend and locker partner, Kerry Thompson, without a flicker of doubt or sarcasm in her voice.

I couldn't blame her for holding that opinion. After all, only a couple of years earlier, she and I used to sneak down to our junior high on Saturday mornings and write flattering junk about ourselves on our own lockers. In erasable grease pencil — we had *some* compassion for the janitor — we'd print stuff like *Garth Girard Loves Lori Laigen* and *Lyon McGuffin thinks Kerry Thompson is a fox!* The guys, supposedly students at Mission Hills High School, were as fake as their names sounded. But our friends didn't know that, and they were totally *impressed*.

Anyway, though we were now freshmen at Mission Hills, how could I blame Kerry for suspecting that this "lucky life" stuff was just another inspired bid for attention? The fact of the matter was, however, I didn't do it.

"I didn't do it," I said to Kerry as I twirled the dial on our combination lock.

She snorted.

"Hey," I said, grabbing my math notebook from the locker and slamming the door, "bragging. Bad luck."

Kerry stared at me for a minute, then nodded. "Gotcha. Sorry. I wonder who did write that on your locker?"

That's one of the things I loved about having had the same best friend since third grade. We had our own private shorthand to communicate with each other. In just four words, I had convinced her that I hadn't written the locker thing by reminding her that to brag about something was unlucky. It could even cost you the thing you were bragging about. Which leads to another huge advantage for being best friends practically forever: Thanks to three million shared experiences, we had the same superstitions.

Kerry and I sauntered down the rapidly filling corridor. Lockers clanged, people sang out greetings, and I was thinking, I wonder who else it is out there who realizes how lucky I am? Because I am, I am, I am. Now see, admitting something like that to yourself isn't bragging — it's simply acknowledging a fact. It becomes bragging only when you say the words aloud, or write them on your locker, or otherwise make them public.

A big, handsome guy with black brush-cut hair was coming our way. "Hey, Lori, how's it going?" he asked, and he waited for me to say "Terrific, Todd," before he moved on.

As we started through the seniors' locker corridor, a sleek blonde in black called out "Coming to my party on Saturday, Lori?" She nodded at Kerry. "You're invited, too," she added politely. "We'll be there, Jade," I answered for both of us.

A few feet further, I was stopped again — this time by Katie Tarantino. "I really need to talk to you for a few minutes tonight, Lori," she said, grabbing my arm. "I'll call you at about eight," I said.

These three exchanges may sound like no big

deal. Until you add in the facts that Todd Killigrew was the captain of the football team, Jade Fontana was the homecoming queen, and Katie Tarantino was the editor of the school paper. Pretty impressive contacts for a lowly freshman, huh?

Dani McDade, head cheerleader, brushed past us with a breezy "Hi, Lori." That she had tossed a wadded-up piece of paper on the top of the notebook I was carrying could have been detected only by either a person with slow-motion eyes or another high-school-newspaper gossip columnist. Which is what I was. Which explains my being invited to A-list parties and being sought out by even the most exalted seniors. And which partially explains the reason I — and at least one other unidentified person — considered my life to be so lucky.

I never tried to kid myself anymore: Landing the columnist job had mostly been a case of being in the right place at the right time. Oh, sure, for a couple of ego-soaring days the previous fall, I'd thought Katie Tarantino had given me such a plum job because of the brilliant satires — or so I had considered them — I'd written back in junior high. (One such gem had been entitled "Santa Claws His Way to the Top.") But I soon learned the truth: Katie had been under intense pressure from Mrs. Caprice, the newspaper's faculty adviser, to beef up readership of the twice-a-month paper among the lowly freshman and sophomores. Hence me, my column, and the strict policy I had to follow: At least half of "Lori's Listening" had to be devoted to people in the ninth and tenth grades.

Kerry glanced at the wad of paper Dani had thrown. "An item for 'Lori's Listening'?" she asked through a yawn.

"Of course," I said, equally nonchalant. I got tips tossed at me all day. Or stuck in my locker. Or written in chalk on the blackboards of classrooms I was due to enter. Or phoned to my home anonymously.

"I bet it's some dirt on Tessa Lord," Kerry said. "I heard someone saw her sneak out to the backyard with Todd Killigrew at Barry Summers' last party."

"It's true," I said. "I saw it. So did a bunch of other people. It serves Dani right. She treats Todd so crummy. Like she screamed at him in front of everybody at the Corvette last Friday just because he said he couldn't go to her house for dinner on Sunday."

"So you're not going to print whatever dirt she's dug up about Tessa?" Kerry asked.

"Depends on what it is." We stopped and I opened the note. Kerry read over my shoulder.

Today in Barclay's fifth-period geometry class, Tessa Lord went to the pencil sharpener, and as she raised her arms her half-slip fell down around her ankles.

Kerry bellowed with laughter, the corkscrews of her wild, dishwater-blonde perm bouncing with delight. I smiled, my tiny little gossip-columnist's mind already busily shaping the tip into a bona fide "Lori's Listening" column item: *Tessa Lord really slipped up in geometry last week when she. . . .*

But I had my doubts about the story. For one thing, half-slips — *any* slips — were not exactly hot items in Southern California. And for another, I distinctly remembered seeing Tessa in the cafeteria at noon, wearing a black leather miniskirt. *Could* she wear a slip under that?

We were about to pass Dani at her locker. I sidled up beside her. "Are you the only one who saw this, or did everybody?" I muttered, barely moving my lips. I had to protect my sources.

"Everybody," she said. "Ask your brother. He was there."

A split second later, we parted.

I was glad to hear I'd be able to confirm the story with another source. If I couldn't, newspaper policy was that the story had to be run as a "blind" item — meaning no names. Example: *What popular blonde songleader really slipped up in geometry last week? It seems she went to the pencil sharpener and soon discovered she had more than just the world at her feet. She found her slip there, too!*

Kerry and I came out of the senior locker corridor into the sunshine and headed past the administration building on our way to the school's front steps.

"What'd she say?" Kerry asked.

"That it happened in front of everyone, including Kevin."

"Speak of the devil." Kerry nodded toward my approaching big, blond brother, who had the usual two to three girls trailing in his wake.

Kevin stopped in front of us. "Need a ride, Lori?" he asked, knowing very well that I didn't. It was his cue that he wanted to shake loose the girls in order to play football or surf with the guys or just be by himself.

"Yeah," I lied. "I have an appointment at Dr. Denton's, and Mom said you have to take me." Now he'd have to load and unload the dishwasher that night, though it was my turn.

Kevin turned to the girls, shaking his head with regret. "Gotta go, ladies." He flashed them his most meltingly charming grin.

They practically sighed all over him, but finally took off. Kevin watched to make sure they didn't go in the direction of the student parking lot where he himself would soon be headed. "Thanks," he said to me as soon as they were out of sight. "I'll load the dishwasher tonight."

"And unload," I said.

He turned to Kerry. "Come on, Ker. I'll drop you home on my way to the beach. There's supposed to be a good south swell today."

"Then your surfboard's in the car?" Kerry asked him.

"Yeah. You'll have to sit in the backseat."

"Home, Jeeves," Kerry said. They headed down the stairs together. "Call me tonight!" Kerry called back to me.

I stood on the front steps and watched them go. A carful of guys drove by on their way out of the student parking lot and directed several loud ah-oohs at me. Which conveniently allows me to introduce what I considered to be the second lucky thing I had going for me on that memorable winter day: I was no longer a 5-foot-7-inch, 98-pound stick figure.

All of my life, I had had the kind of looks that prompted people to say "Someday, Lori, you're going to be quite a knockout." That was because I had thick black hair and grass-green eyes but the kind of body only Pinocchio could love: all knobs and joints and sticks. One creep of a distant relative had observed that when I walked I always looked like I was about to topple over. In junior high, the kids had called me "Lori Laigs," or, worse, "Skeeny Laigs."

"Hey, don't knock it," my mom had said when I'd told her about the nicknames. "In ten years, when all of your friends are complaining about thunder thighs, you'll be thanking your lucky stars that you have such nice, long, thin legs."

Well, as it turned out, I was thanking my lucky stars in what was closer to ten *months*. Sure, I still had those toothpick legs, but the rest of me had grown to balance things out. For example, I wasn't flat-chested anymore. And no longer did my mother — under a vow of secrecy — have to order my panties from the girls' section of the Sears catalog.

Yes, on that day, January 14th of last year, it could be said that I was . . . well, not *ecstatic* about my looks, but at least satisfied. Especially when I was wearing something new, like the soft, coral-colored angora sweater I had on over my jeans. All day long, people had been remarking that it was the same color as my cheeks (which had had a little help from a blusher brush).

I looked up when I heard a couple of throaty-sounding beeps of a horn. Finally! I flew down the stairs toward an ancient Chevy Impala. I stuck my head in the window and stuck my tongue out at the last — but certainly not the least — of my lucky charms: B.G. Grimes. I just called him "Big Guy."

" 'Bout time, Big Guy," I said, getting in and slamming the door.

"The guys still had it in a million pieces on the floor of the shop," he said. Big Guy had been parking his car in the school auto shop all week, getting the engine overhauled. He smiled at me as if he hadn't seen me in three weeks. I loved it. I slid next to him across the quaint bench seat, kissed his cheek, and stayed there, like girls did in those corny old Annette Funicello beach movies.

Big Guy turned left onto Mission Hills Boulevard. I snuggled happily beside him, glancing up at his face about every thirteen seconds just because I could never get used to how good-looking he was. Auburn hair, dark tan, blue eyes — such a strange color combination, but it worked. Big Guy was also a big guy, but not, at the moment, as bulked out as he allowed himself to get in the fall, when he was Mission Hills High School's star halfback. I mean, he had an identifiable neck in the other three seasons.

At the first stoplight, he took his hand off

the steering wheel and squeezed one of mine. "If I was driving south from L.A. at 65 miles per hour, and you — "

I cut him off with a groan. "Wait'll we get to my house! Can't I even have a ten-minute break between school and tutoring?"

"You probably hung out on the front steps for at least ten minutes. That was your break."

I sighed. "Let's just take a fast cruise down to San Diego Bay and back. Fifteen minutes max. Then I'll spout algebraic equations until you scream for mercy. I promise."

"Uh-uh. Your mom might be out doing errands. She might see us. Then you wouldn't be able to go to Jade Fontana's party on Saturday night." I was not allowed to drive anywhere but to or from school with Big Guy unless I practically had written permission two weeks in advance. "Look, let's get the tutoring out of the way, and then we'll walk over to the park," he said. "Or we'll ask your mom if we can drive over to McDonald's."

I sighed again, defeated.

"Where was I?" Big Guy asked. "Oh, yeah. If I was driving south from L.A. on Interstate 5 at 65 miles an hour and you were driving north from San Diego on 5 at 45 miles per hour, in which beach town would we probably pass each other?"

That's an example of one of the less obvious reasons I loved being tutored by Big Guy. None of this "If Train X is traveling 200 miles an hour and Train Y is traveling 100 . . ." and blah-blah-blah. He used real-life examples . . . well, *almost* real-life, since at age fourteen, of course, I couldn't drive yet and no one drives 45 on a Southern California freeway by choice. But even his semi-real-life examples made algebra 800 times X times Y more interesting and more understandable than Mr. Barclay ever made it.

I shot him an admiring glance as I opened my notebook to jot down the figures he'd given me. And I started thinking about luck again. Incredible as it seems, even the one black cloud that had appeared on my horizon during that freshman year of mine — the fact that I was failing algebra — had turned out to have a silver lining. Barclay had assigned Big Guy as a tutor. Before too many twice-weekly tutoring sessions had gone by, X had fallen for Y. And Y was equally wild about X.

We pulled up in front of my house.

"San Clemente," I said, getting out.

"Right!" Big Guy said, following me up the driveway. "Now we'll work on percentages. When your brother Kevin ran for junior class vice-president, he won 817 votes, which was

95 percent of the votes cast. How many students voted?"

My mother called out and waved at me from the doorway of the house next door, an ancient, Spanish-style, hacienda-type thing with one of those red-tile roofs that have been all the rage in California for about the last 300 years. I waved back rather absently, trying to figure Big Guy's problem in my head. The moving van in the driveway of that house didn't even register. I'm talking about the moving van that moved the Marshes to Mission Hills and made a miserable mess of Lori Laigen's lucky life.

Chapter 2

"860," I said, looking up from my notebook. "860 people voted."

"Right," Big Guy said. He put his feet up on the ottoman. We were sitting in the family room. "What's the equation you used to find the answer?"

"817 over X equals 95 over 100."

"Very good."

"Arf, arf," I barked.

My mother came through the family room wearing her usual workday outfit — a faded kelly-green velour jogging suit. "New family moving in next door."

"Temporarily, no doubt," I said. I turned to Big Guy. "The Navy owns that house and rents it out to officers who get transferred here."

"Well, they're Navy all right, but they're buying the place," my mom said. "The father is planning to retire from the Navy in a year or so. The whole family has fallen in love with San Diego, so they're here to stay. Hallelujah! Now maybe we can start a Neighborhood Watch program on this end of the block."

"We've already got a Neighborhood Watch, Mom," I said. "You."

She stuck her tongue out at me. "Anyway, they've got four girls, and one of them is your age, Lori."

"Four girls? *Little Women*," I snickered.

Big Guy looked at me questioningly.

"That's a book — a classic by Louisa May Alcott," I explained.

"Oh, yeah," he said. "I've heard of it."

"I thought of *Little Women*, too," my mom said. "I mean, this new family's name is Marsh, same as the family in the book."

I shook my head, yawning. "The family in the book is named *March*. I ought to know. I must have read it ten times."

The look Big Guy threw me was pure admiration. It was the same sort of look he got from me whenever I caught him checking out math puzzle books from the library or watching stuff about apes on PBS just for the fun of it. We never really talked about it, but our relationship was very much based on a sort of right brain/left brain, opposites-attract equation. He considered me a literary whiz kid; I had him pegged as a math/science genius. About the only subject we were both passionately interested in was astronomy. Since I'd met him, we'd probably spent 100 hours at the Palomar Observatory and/or the Reuben H. Fleet Space Theater happily turning into star-nerds the instant we walked through the doors.

"Didn't you have to read *Little Women* in Toffler's freshman English class?" I asked Big Guy now.

"Nope. We got to choose from a bunch of classics. I picked *Withering Heights*."

"Wuthering," I said. "Sounds like you found it truly memorable."

He laughed lazily.

My mother headed for the little room off the family room that she uses for an office. She's a freelance graphic designer.

She sighed. "Well, back to the Potter Porta-Pet Potty brochure."

"A pretty putrid prospect?" I asked.

"Positively," she replied. "Pete Potter's a persnickety, penny-pinching perfectionist." She turned around in the doorway. "Oh, I forgot. There was a message on the answering machine for you. Something about how a Hillary Deschamps and her family will be 'summering in Switzerland,' quote unquote. Want to hear it?"

I frowned. That answering machine was supposed to be for my mother's business calls only, and it said so right on the tape. "No. Everybody knows that I do not accept tips that are left on the machine. Did it sound like a boy or a girl?"

"It sounded like a girl trying to sound like a boy."

"Hillary herself, no doubt," I said with a sigh.

Big Guy snapped his fingers at me. "Okay, you, back to work. If Sears came to your mom and wanted her to design a 360-page catalog — "

"She'd tell Pete Potter where to put his Porta-Pet Potties," my mom said as she closed her office door.

Big Guy laughed. "If Sears wanted twice as many black-and-white pages as color, and they had. . . ." He trailed off as I waved my hands at him.

"Did you hear that?" I whispered. It had been a barely discernible scratching sound . . . no, a tapping noise . . . actually, a sort of combination tapping/scratching. And it had come from the living room. But it had stopped.

"I don't hear anything," Big Guy said impatiently, flipping through my math textbook. Then it started again. This time, he did hear it. He narrowed his eyes and turned an ear toward the living room. "Sounds like a mouse."

Instinctively, my feet flew up onto the ottoman next to Big Guy's.

"No . . . wait," he said, still listening hard as the noise stopped and then started again. "I think it's coming from the front door. Maybe Mr. Crank wants in." Mr. Crank is our Siamese cat.

"Mr. Crank simply screeches when he wants in," I said, jumping up and heading for the front door. I threw it open. There was a girl with long, reddish-brown hair standing there, and she leaped back in alarm. She had brown doe eyes that looked huge and frightened in her thin, pale face. And she had the thinnest, whitest neck I'd ever seen.

"Oh, I'm so terribly sorry!" she said, her hand at her mouth. She had a very sweet, high, almost Minnie Mouse voice.

I bit my lip. What was she apologizing for? I was the one who had nearly given her a heart attack. "I'm sorry, too," I said. "I thought it was some stray animal scratching at the — " I broke off, embarrassed. What an insult!

But she didn't seem offended. To the contrary. "Oh, that was *me*," she said. "I'm so sorry to bother you. You see, your mother said she worked at home, and I figured if I knocked softly enough, I wouldn't disturb her . . . that someone else who wasn't busy would hear me. Oh, but now I see that I must have disturbed *you* and I'm so sorry — "

"What can I do for you?" I interrupted. How many times could a person say she was sorry in about 52 seconds?

Suddenly, the girl smiled. She had a very sweet smile. "Oh, I'm sorry! I forgot to introduce myself. I'm Bethanny Marsh. My family just moved in next door." She put out her hand and I shook it. Her hand was small and soft.

"I was wondering if I could make a quick phone call," Bethanny said. "Our phone won't be connected until tomorrow, and your mom said we should feel free to come over and use yours. But if now is not a good time . . . I don't want to inconvenience anyone. . . ."

"It's no problem," I said. "Come on in." I introduced myself as she followed me through the living room and into the family room, where I introduced her to Big Guy. I pointed to the phone on the table next to the couch.

"Want us to clear out for a couple of minutes?" Big Guy asked her.

"Oh, no! Oh, please don't leave on my account," Bethanny cried, perching on the edge of the couch. "I would just feel terrible."

I sat down on the arm of the chair Big Guy was sitting in.

She took a slip of paper from the pocket of her wool skirt, picked up the receiver, and with delicate jabs punched in a number. "Is this Western Union?" she asked after a few seconds. "Good. I'd like to send a telegram to Captain J. Marsh." She read an Arabic-sounding address off the slip of paper. "He's stationed aboard a ship in the Persian Gulf," she explained to me and Big Guy and whoever was on the other end of the line. "Okay, here's the message: 'House perfect. All are happy, fine, moved in. Miss you. Love and kisses. Bethanny.' " She covered the receiver. "Daddy worries so much about us . . . the telegram should help." She uncovered the mouthpiece. "How much will that be, please? . . . Oh, that's just fine. I've saved up enough allowance to cover that. Will it be too much trouble to send me the bill?" She recited her name and address, hung up, and turned to us with her sweet smile.

Just then, Mr. Crank marched haughtily into the room.

"Ooh!" Bethanny squealed. "A Siamese! May I hold him?" She headed for him.

"At your own risk," I said. "He not only

scratches, he bites. We don't call him Mr. Crank for nothing."

But to my shock, when Bethanny leaned halfway over, Mr. Crank actually sort of leaped into her arms. "I've never seen him do that before," I said. "What are you wearing? Eau de Catnip?"

Bethanny giggled. "No. We have four cats of our own. He probably smells them on me."

Within seconds, a harsh, rusty sound emanated from Mr. Crank. He was purring as loud as a garbage truck.

"You really have a knack with cats, Bethanny," Big Guy said.

"Yes, you do, my deah, since I never even knew that particular creature had purr capabilities," I said in my veddy snootiest voice.

"I just love cats," Bethanny said. "Maybe Mr. Crank will make friends with ours."

"He'd make a pretty catty friend," I said, laughing merrily. Big Guy joined me.

Bethanny stared at us, puzzled. "Catty?" she said, pronouncing the word as if she'd never heard it before.

"You know — mean, malicious," I explained. "Mr. Crank is not exactly Mr. Sociable with other cats, as those various scars on his ears and legs will attest." Inwardly, I groaned. Sometimes the way I talked sounded too much like the way I wrote up tips for my gossip column. Too, too Rona Barrett-ish.

Bethanny continued to look puzzled. "How did they ever get a word like that from such sweet, harmless creatures?" she asked, rubbing her chin against Mr. Crank's head. Mr. Crank gave me a mean, triumphant look, knowing that Bethanny couldn't see it.

I asked her what grade she was in, and it turned out she was a freshman, like me. She said she'd be attending Mission Hills High School, as would her sister Joanne, a sophomore. Another sister was going to a different high school, and the fourth was still in junior high.

"I really feel bad that I won't be starting school at the beginning of the semester," Bethanny said.

"Yeah, you'll have a lot of catching up to do," I said. "What a drag. There's enough homework as it is, without having to do a lot of catch-up stuff on top of it."

"Oh, no, it's not *me* I'm worried about," Bethanny said. "It's the teachers I feel sorry for. It's so hard for them when there's a new student in the class. They have to keep going back and explaining things just for that one person."

When Bethanny left, a few minutes and several profuse speeches of gratitude later, I turned to Big Guy. "Is she for real?"

He laughed, stood up, and kissed me lightly. "Let's call it a day on the tutoring and go for a walk."

On our way out, we passed by Mr. Crank, perched on a table so he could see out our front window. Still purring loudly, he was watching Bethanny pick flowers in her new front yard.

"Oh, can it, you big phony," I said. "You can't fool me. Quit pretending you've suddenly turned into the Mr. Rogers of the neighborhood. You are and always will be Mr. Crank."

The next morning, Kerry stopped by my house, as always, and we set off on our usual leisurely walk to school. That morning's topic of conversation was a tearjerker movie she and I had watched on TV the night before. The stars had been Raquel Welch and Michael Gross, who plays the father on *Family Ties*.

We were about two blocks from my house when we turned a corner and saw Bethanny Marsh walking ahead of us. "Oh, Kerry, that's my new neighbor," I said. "Let's catch up with her, and I'll introduce you. She's our age."

Bethanny stopped and turned to us with her

please-like-me and/or forgive-me smile when I called out to her. She was wearing one of those lacy, high-necked, Victorian-style blouses with big, cuffed sleeves and a cameo at her throat. She was also wearing jeans and Reeboks. It was a cute . . . no, a *sweet*-looking outfit.

"Isn't it a glorious day?" she cried after I introduced her to Kerry.

The drippy fog was so thick you couldn't see more than a half a block ahead. Kerry shot me a sidewise look. "It is, if you like fog, and your hair doesn't frizz," she grumped. People who were overly cheerful first thing in the morning had always annoyed her.

Bethanny looked dashed.

I tried to make up for Kerry's crankiness. "Where's your sister, Bethanny? The one who'll be a sophomore at school?"

"Joanne? Oh . . . she rides her bike to school. When we lived in San Francisco, I rode my bike to school, too. But it used to make Joanne mad, because I couldn't keep up with her very well, and she sort of felt like she had to stick with me. I just couldn't make it up some of those hills without getting off and walking. Then, one morning, I fell off my bike and broke my ankle. And I felt so bad! I mean, I made Joanne late for school."

Kerry thought Bethanny was being sarcastic-funny, so she laughed. Until she caught Bethanny's puzzled expression. Then she broke off mid-laugh.

I changed the subject. "Did you see that movie last night about the woman who had that awful disease?" I asked Bethanny.

She shook her head, but winced. "She doesn't die, does she? Oh, please, forget I asked. Don't tell me! I can't bear it when. . . ." She put her hands over her ears and mumbled something.

Just then, Kerry and I heard a familiar hiss, and we flew off the sidewalk and into the street a split second before somebody's automatic sprinklers whooshed on full-force. Probably because she had her ears covered, Bethanny's reflexes weren't as good. By the time she made it to the street, squealing, one sleeve and one pant leg were pretty well drenched.

We saw a woman standing in the front window of the house with the sprinklers.

"You don't own the sidewalk!" Kerry shouted at her. "Keep your water off the sidewalk!"

Bethanny tugged at Kerry's arm. "Oh, please, don't shout at that poor old lady! I'm all right. And anyway, it was my own fault. I shouldn't have dawdled when I saw you two take off."

Kerry slapped her forehead, clearly exasperated with Bethanny.

When we reached the corner of that block, Kerry stopped. "Well, Bethanny, this is where we wait every day for our friend . . . uh . . . Raquel Gross. You'd better go on. Raquel sometimes oversleeps, and we don't want to make you late for school on your first day."

So Bethanny ended up going on without us. As soon as she was out of earshot, we burst out laughing.

"Raquel . . . Gross?" I sputtered.

"Sure. That's what you'd get if Raquel Welch married Michael Gross and decided not to keep her own name."

"Sounds gross," I said. "What's the real reason you wanted to ditch Bethanny?"

"I just couldn't take another minute of her," Kerry said. "She's just so horribly *sweet*. I think I got two cavities just from being within six feet of her."

"Well, I wouldn't want to be with her every minute of every day, but I think she's sort of refreshing," I found myself saying, to my surprise. "I mean, it's kind of nice for a change being around someone who always puts other people first."

Kerry shrieked, grabbed me by the shoulders, and shook me playfully. "Oh, no, Bethanny's trying to take possession of your body! Help this girl! It's like the invasion of the pod people or something."

We laughed and walked a half block in silence.

"Didn't Bethanny say there's another one?" Kerry finally asked. "A sister? Ugh. *Double* ugh."

"I've only met Bethanny so far, but there are actually four sisters altogether."

"The Saccharine Sisters," Kerry snickered.

I shook my head slowly. "No, saccharine implies fake," I said. "And I'm pretty sure Bethanny's for real."

Chapter 3

Ms. Toffler is one of the nicest teachers in the entire U.S.A.

I sat there staring at the little slip of paper. Whoever had submitted it had originally written *Ms. Toffler is the nicest teacher in the entire U.S.A.* but had gone back and inserted the words "one of" as if he/she didn't want to hurt the feelings of the eight million other American teachers. Who would have written such a thing and put it in my locker? Certainly not Ms. Toffler. She was too straightforward, too honest to secretly submit the thing on her own. And anyway, it was accepted fact, not gossip that Ms. Toffler was the nicest teacher at school. So why had someone bothered to submit it as gossip? Talk about boring moves.

Sighing, I tossed the tip on the pile of others I'd found in my locker at noon and glanced at the clock on the wall of the newspaper office. Three minutes to three. Other staff members were filing into the room and taking their places around me at the big table we used for our regular Wednesday-afternoon staff meetings.

I said a few hellos and opened up the next tip.

Janica Sorenson doesn't know it yet, but she went out last Saturday night not with her boyfriend, Scott Tinsdale, but with his identical twin, Sam. I heard that Scott pulled the secret switch because —

"Who's in charge here?"

I looked up at the sound of the voice, annoyed to be interrupted in the middle of such a juicy tip.

The voice belonged to a tall girl wearing a startlingly bright fuchsia sweater that looked great with her long, smoky-brown hair. She was deeply tanned and had big, dark eyes that were narrowed thoughtfully as they circled the table.

She threw a well-worn canvas backpack full of books on the table, scattering my tips everywhere.

"Hey!" I protested.

"Who's in charge here?" she said again, hands on her hips.

"I am. I'm the editor." Katie Tarantino had

just come through the door. She took her place at the head of the table, her eyes fixed on the newcomer.

The tall girl laughed. "Aha! I am finally going to meet the one, the only female to have a position of influence at this school."

"*What?*" Kate practically squeaked. "What on earth are you talking about?"

"Or, wait a minute," the girl continued. "Maybe yours isn't really a position of influence. Maybe you're merely their puppet. When they say 'Jump' do you say 'How high'?"

A wave of irritation flickered across Katie's face. "Who, may I ask, are *they*?"

The girl threw her thick, shiny hair over her shoulder impatiently. "The men at this school. Listen, in the one day I've been here, I've met a handful of student body officers, several jocks, and an assortment of other such crowd-gatherers, and not a one of them was of the female persuasion. So the way I figure it, they tossed you this crumb — this editor's position — just to keep the accusations of sexism in check."

Katie was really angry now. Even her ears were red. "Listen, I don't know who you are, but you are full of it. I got this position based on my work on the newspaper for the last two years. And I was appointed by Mrs. Caprice, not *they*, whoever *they* are!"

The dark-haired newcomer's eyes darted across the room to where Mrs. Caprice, the faculty adviser to the paper, was busily writing in a notebook. She always pretended not to be listening at our staff meetings. But you could tell by subsequent conversations with her that she had heard every word, probably even wrote it all down.

"Well, hey, right on, Ms. Caprice!" the girl said. "That's the spirit. We have to stick together if we ever want to get anywhere in this world."

Brian Cranston, who wrote most of the sports stuff, groaned. "Listen, isn't radical feminism sort of out of style? I mean, *Ms.* magazine is older than we are. So give it a rest, will you?"

The girl leaned across the table until her face was maybe six inches from Brian's. "What's the matter? Do you feel threatened?"

Well, yes, Brian obviously did. He reared back in his seat and kept his mouth shut from then on.

"Anyway, Katie's not the only female at this school to have a powerful position," said Deena Fishman. "There's also . . . um . . ." Helplessly, she looked around the table at the rest of us girls. I frantically racked my brain but I couldn't come up with anyone, either. Nor could the rest of the girls.

"I . . . uh . . . guess she's right," Deena muttered.

Mrs. Caprice hurried over to the table. "Meet Joanne Marsh, people. She's a sophomore whose family just moved to Mission Hills, and she's asked to join the staff."

My mouth dropped open. *This* girl was sweet little Bethanny's sister?

"Joanne will be signing on for now as a general assignment reporter until a position opens up," Mrs. Caprice rushed on. "She's done a lot of writing and was editor of the paper at her old school in San Francisco."

It was Katie's turn to look threatened. "Well, I've already made out my assignments list for the next edition," she snapped. "And there are no stories left for you to cover, Joanne. So sorry."

Joanne dropped into a chair, grinning. "No problem. Maybe I'll just whip out a freelance essay or two for you. See if you like them."

Suddenly, I saw that Kerry was standing in the doorway, waving to get my attention. I got up and went over to her.

She put some wadded-up pieces of paper in

my hands. "Found some more tips in our locker after the final bell and thought you might need them," she whispered. "Didn't you say Katie sometimes asks to see them before you rough out a first draft?"

"Yeah, but she won't bother today. She's got her hands full."

Kerry stifled a giggle. "So I see. Who *is* that?" She nodded toward Joanne.

"That," I whispered, "is one of your Saccharine Sisters!"

I walked home from school that day alone, like I always did on Wednesdays after the newspaper meetings. Kerry never felt like waiting around that long. And Big Guy worked at his mom's antique shop on Goldfinch Street after school on Wednesdays, since her full-time employee took Wednesdays off.

As I turned the corner onto our street, I spotted Bethanny in the Marshes' front yard, playing with a couple of kittens. Mr. Crank was sitting in our front window, looking on jealously. He definitely had a crush on Bethanny.

"How was your first day of school?" I asked, stopping at the hedge that separated our houses.

"Wonderful! I guess it could have been pretty intimidating since the school is so big and everything, but one of the teachers really helped me out. She helped me find my locker, walked me to my homeroom, and even introduced me to a whole bunch of people. Ms. Toffler is just the nicest teacher in the entire world and — " Bethanny broke off and blushed the color of watermelon chunks.

"Seems like I've heard that before," I said lightly, but decided against giving her a hard time about the gossip-column tip. The kid deserved a break on her first day of school and all. "I met Joanne today, in the newspaper office," I said.

Her eyes filled with gratitude because I'd changed the subject. "Oh, I'm so glad."

"She's nothing like you."

"None of us is like the other. Daddy says that's what makes our life together so interesting. Want to meet my other sisters? Megan and Amanda?"

I nodded. Bethanny scooped up the kittens, and I followed her around the house to the backyard. There we came upon a girl stretched out under a palm tree. Another girl, sitting several feet away on a patio chair, was hunched over a sketchbook.

"That's Amanda, our youngest sister," Bethanny said, pointing at the girl who was sketching, "and Megan, who's the oldest. Hey, you guys, this is our neighbor, Lori Laigen."

Megan, under the tree, smiled at me and halfway raised an arm to wave.

"Don't move, Megan!" Amanda called sharply. "I'm doing your hands right this second." She glanced up at me briefly. "Hi." She had a mouthful of braces.

Amanda was smaller than the other Marsh girls. She was pretty, with butter-blonde hair and sky-blue eyes. But it was Megan, posing under the palm tree, who was the real stunning beauty. Somehow, she had gotten all of the best features of the other Marsh girls: the texture and luxuriance of Joanne's hair; Bethanny's perfect creamy complexion; and Amanda's blondeness and big blue eyes. Plus, Megan had a couple of attributes that were hers alone. She had a gorgeous body. And she was obviously proud of it, since she wore skintight jeans and a sweater that looked spray-painted on, to borrow one of my mother's favorite descriptions.

"Okay, Meggie, take five," Amanda said, dropping her pencil and flexing her fingers.

Megan stood up with a sigh of relief and wriggled a mirror out of her back pocket. "Oh, look, I'm sweating a little!" she cried in the same tone anyone else would have said "Oh, look, my pet has died!"

"You're so vain!" Amanda sang.

"Well, sweat makes my mascara run, and when that happens I look sort of tired and washed out," Megan said. "Look, you're going to have to finish without me, Amanda. I've got to go in and redo my makeup. I met a couple of guys at school today who said they'd drop by this afternoon, and I can't let them see me like this. They'd absolutely *run*."

"No!" Amanda wailed. "You can't leave yet. At least let me finish your hand. Just hold it up right there for a minute, okay? I can do it that way." Feverishly, she went at the sketchbook again as Megan — heaving a mighty put-upon sigh — did as she was asked.

Just then, Joanne came around the corner of the house, carrying her backpack and walking a bicycle.

"Meeting the troops, huh?" she said cheerfully with a brisk nod at me. She wheeled the bike into the garage.

"Where do you go to school, Megan?" I asked. "How come you don't go to Mission Hills?"

"I go to Point Loma High School," she said, "because they have a special course on becoming a flight attendant."

"Most people become flight attendants for the travel perks," Joanne called from the garage. "But Megan just wants to hook herself a rich guy flying first class, so she can retire from the human race." Joanne's voice was full of disdain.

Megan laughed a low, delighted laugh, as if Joanne had paid her a supreme compliment. Something told me that Megan wasn't exactly Mensa material. And that Joanne hadn't been kidding about Megan's goal. Joanne strode past us and went into the house.

"There goes Miss Sociable," Amanda snapped.

"Let's make that *Ms*. Sociable," Joanne called out one of the windows.

"Joanne's probably just tired today, Amanda," Bethanny said. "The first day of school can be stressful." She turned to me. "When Amanda graduates from junior high, she's not going to Mission Hills, either, just like Megan doesn't. Amanda's going to Patrick Henry High, where they have a special program for talented young artists."

I stared at Bethanny for a minute. I had a very strange, undescribable feeling . . . like there was something I'd forgotten to ask her . . . or that there was something I'd missed . . . or was it just one of those weird *déjà vu* things?

* * *

A few minutes later, I walked into our house, still feeling vaguely troubled.

My mom came out of her office. "I thought I heard you over at the Marshes."

I nodded. "Now I've met all of them except for the parents. What a weird assortment."

The faint tinkling of a piano drifted through the front windows. "Weird but talented," my mom said. "Bethanny plays a pretty mean piano from what I've heard. And Peggy Marsh, the mother, told me that Joanne's already had a story published in one of the teen magazines, and that Amy, who's only twelve, has won some art awards."

"It's Amanda, not Amy," I said. "You're thinking of the book, Mom." And that's when it hit me. I grabbed my mom's arms. "Oh, that's *it*, Mom! *That's* what's been bugging me!"

"What are you talking about?"

"Remember yesterday how we were comparing the Marsh family with the March family in *Little Women*?"

She nodded.

"Well, don't you see? They have even more in common than we thought. This is really *weird* . . . but really interesting. Look at how simliar their names are to the girls in the book. They're even just about the same ages. Megan and Meg, Joanne and Jo, Bethanny and Beth, Amanda and Amy. Weird, weird, *weird*."

My mom laughed. "Hey, you're right. I bet the Marshes did it on purpose. Maybe *Little Women* was Peggy's favorite childhood book or something."

"Well, that probably explains the names, but look at how much the girls even sort of look and act like their respective characters in the book," I said thoughtfully, shaking my head. "That just has to be pure, weird coincidence. Joanne's kind of a feminist writer type like Jo was. Amanda and Amy — talented in art. Megan and Meg? Gorgeous bimbos. Complete airheads. And Bethanny and Beth are your basic all-around saints. If I'm remembering right, Beth in the book even plays the piano and has a thing about cats."

Just then the doorbell rang, and we went together to answer it. A middle-aged woman with Bethanny's sweet smile stood on our doorstep. This had to be Peggy Marsh.

My mother introduced us. Mrs. Marsh seemed as kindhearted and warm as Bethanny, and she even had the same Minnie Mouse voice, but she was about 300 percent more assertive than her third daughter.

"May I use your phone, Sue?" she asked briskly, not hesitating a second as my mother held the door open and gestured her inside. "It turns out the phone company can't come till tomorrow afternoon, so I'll have to cancel Amanda's orthodontist appointment and stay at home."

My mother led Mrs. Marsh into the family room and pointed to the phone.

"I should have done this earlier, but we were just so busy at the hospital this afternoon," Mrs. Marsh said.

"Are you a doctor or nurse?" I asked her.

"No. Just a volunteer."

She called the orthodontist and rescheduled Amanda's appointment. "Now let's see, what else still needs to be done today?" she asked herself as she hung up the phone.

"Mrs. Marsh — " I began.

"Please call me Peggy, sweetheart," she said.

"Peggy, did you read *Little Women* when you were younger? Is that where you got your daughters' names?"

She headed for the front door. "No, honey, I never read that book," she said absently. "I grew up in England, so naturally they had us reading the English classics in school. Now, let's see, I need to run to the supermarket, start on the Save the Whales mailing . . . Thanks, Sue . . . Nice to meet you, Lori . . .

Finish sewing the collar on Megan's blouse." She went through the little opening in the hedge that separated our house from the Marshes' and disappeared.

"Well," I said to my mother, "she never read it. That makes the *Little Women* connections even more of a coincidence."

I went up to my room and called Kerry to tell her about it. "I'm thinking of writing it up as an item for my next column," I finished. "It's sort of cute."

Kerry yawned. "Nah. Don't waste the space. Who knows how many people at school have read *Little Women*? Probably not that many. And anyway, the Marshes are new. Nobody knows them."

I laughed. "I have a feeling it won't be long before Joanne is pretty well-known around school."

"Hey, right on, sister!" Kerry said in a Joanne voice.

Then we started talking about how Scott Tinsdale palmed his girlfriend Janica off on his twin brother, and I forgot all about the little women next door.

Chapter 4

Several days went by in which I didn't run into any of the Marsh girls, though nearly every day, both before and after school, I'd see at least one guy pull into their driveway, looking for Megan.

One Tuesday afternoon, after our algebra tutoring session, Big Guy and I sat cuddling in the family room. He was watching an old *Star Trek* episode while I opened up the day's gossip column tips.

B.G. Grimes saved Sandy Manson from serious injury after school on Monday. Sandy was coming down the East Wing stairs and tripped. B.G. caught her so that she suffered only a bruise from falling against the handrail. Then B.G. helped her to the nurse's office. Charlotte McSween, school nurse, said B.G. saved Sandy from a broken leg or worse.

"My hero," I snickered. "But hey, Big Guy, I can't run this. Everybody knows you're my boyfriend. It would look like self-promotion."

He sat up straight and withdrew the arm that had been slung over my shoulders. "What are you talking about?"

I handed him the tip. "And anyway, this isn't column material," I said. "It's too blah. It'd be different if you had tripped Sandy on purpose, or if she was my rival for your affections, so to speak. Or something like that."

Big Guy read the tip and shook his head. "I didn't write this."

I looked at him closely and believed him. "Then who did, I wonder."

"Maybe Sandy Manson did."

"I sincerely doubt it," I said. "If I had tripped over my own two feet, I wouldn't want any publicity on it."

Big Guy snapped his fingers. "Wait a minute. I just remembered something. You know who was working in the nurse's office when I took Sandy there?"

Suddenly, he didn't even have to tell me. "Bethanny Marsh," I said.

"Yeah. The girl next door who came over to use the phone when I was here last week. But I don't think she even noticed Sandy and me come into the nurse's office. I mean, she was busy taking the temperature of a guy lying on one of the beds, a guy who looked green and ready to barf. And she was talking to him, too. So I guess it probably wasn't her who wrote the tip."

"Believe me, it was," I said with a sigh and without a doubt. "So Bethanny's working in the nurse's office. Well, knowing her, it comes as no surprise." I tossed the tip on the "rejects" pile and went on to the next.

That evening, my mom, dad, Kevin, and I were sitting around the dining room table, shooting the breeze over dessert, when the doorbell rang.

Kevin went to answer it and came back with a very distraught Peggy Marsh and a stouter, older, sterner-looking version of Joanne. Peggy introduced the other woman as her sister-in-law, "Aunt Marsh."

"Oh, Sue, Bill, . . . my husband has come down with a terrible case of dengue fever and I'm going to Kuwait to be with him," Peggy said to my parents, wringing her hands.

"Dengue fever? That's terrible," said my dad, who is a doctor. "I don't think there's been a case of that in the U.S. for thirty years. But the Middle East . . . well, that's certainly a different story."

"He's too sick to be brought home, and . . .

oh, Bill, will you keep an eye on things over at our house?" Peggy asked him. "I don't know how long I'll be gone . . . and Aunt Marsh has graciously consented to stay with the girls . . . but I'd feel much better knowing that a man was looking in on — "

"Peggy, you nip that kind of talk in the bud right this instant," the aunt boomed. "We are perfectly capable of taking care of ourselves, thank you very much. Now that's that." It was easy to see that Joanne's feminism had a genetic root.

Peggy's lips trembled. "But — "

"You heard me, Peg. Now let's get going. You have a lot of packing to do, and I want you to do it now, so you can get a good night's sleep. You've got a twenty-hour day ahead of you." Aunt Marsh took Peggy's arm and propelled her out of the dining room toward the front door.

My dad started after them. "Don't worry, Peggy, we'll keep an eye on things," he said. Aunt Marsh whipped her head around and aimed a withering look at my dad. He stopped in his tracks. We heard the front door open and close. My dad came back to the table and laughed nervously. "Aunt Bossy."

"More like Sergeant Marsh," Kevin said, grinning.

But my mom was upset. "What about *Captain* Marsh? What's dengue fever, Bill? It sounds horrible."

"It's spread by mosquitoes," my dad said. He launched into one of his full-fledged, medical lingo, Greek-to-me explanations. I just sat there, numbed out, as something gnawed at me. It was the same sort of vague, troubled feeling I'd had a week earlier, after I'd met Megan and Amanda in the Marshes' yard.

When dinner was over, I went up to my bedroom and paced, racking my brain for inspiration. What was bothering me? Aside from finding out that Captain Marsh was very sick, why had Peggy's visit left me feeling so frustrated . . . so . . . so . . . *anxious*?

Finally, I took *Little Women* out of my bookcase and flopped down across my bed with it. For my whole life, I'd used my favorite books sort of like medicine. Whenever I felt angry or hurt or lonesome or depressed, I would just pick up an old favorite and sort of crawl between the lines, to bask cozily, comfortingly, in simpler times, or at least among someone else's problems. Reading an old friend — because that's what each book felt like — always made me feel better. I chose *Little Women* that night simply because I'd been thinking about it off and on since the Marshes moved in.

I opened the book to page one, line one:

"Christmas won't be Christmas without any presents," grumbled Jo, lying on the rug.

And then I read straight through to the end, though I skipped over large parts that were mostly description or trivial action. But for once in my life, *Little Women* wasn't soothing. No, with each page, that vague, troubled feeling I'd had earlier crystallized into a certain, deepening dread.

When I finished the book, I called Kerry, even though it was midnight.

"Kerry!" I gasped. "You have to come over here before school tomorrow . . . early. *You have to!* Oh, Kerry, come at six-thirty, okay?"

"No way!" she said crankily, sleepily. "I'm not getting up at six. Especially when you woke me up at midnight. A person has to get some sleep, you know."

"Kerry," I said tearfully, "you be here at six-thirty. Otherwise, you and I will have to live with the responsibility of someone's death for the rest of our lives!"

Kerry arrived on our doorstep at six twenty-two the next morning.

"I wasn't sure if I dreamed that you called last night or not," she said, yawning. But once we got up to my room and she got a good look at my pale face and red eyes, she knew she hadn't been dreaming. "What was all that about somebody dying?" she asked, wide-eyed.

I sat her down on my bed and filled her in about how Mrs. Marsh and her sister-in-law had come over to tell us about Captain Marsh's dengue fever.

"Oh, that's really sad," Kerry said. "But pardon me for being so callous . . . you've never even met the guy. Even if he dies from this dengue stuff — and that would be terrible — well, I can't understand why you're having a nervous breakdown about it."

"It's not the father I'm worried about," I said, starting to cry again. "It's Bethanny."

"*Bethanny?* Now look, Lori, her mom certainly isn't going to let her go over to Egypt or wherever the guy is so she can catch this weird disease that — "

"Would you stop being so incredibly dense?" I shouted. "Don't you remember the book?" I leaped up, went over to my bookcase, extracted *Little Women* from it, and threw it in Kerry's lap.

She picked it up and glanced idly at the cover. "You are really freaked out. Would you care to explain yourself?"

"Look, I'll just lay it on the line for you.

We've got to make friends with Bethanny, and we've got to do it right away. Today. This morning, even."

"Why?" Kerry demanded. "We'd be risking sugar overload. Even diabetic coma. I can't *stand* her. She's in my cooking class and *nobody* can be that sweet all the time. I bet she goes up to her room at night, closes the door, and screams obscenities at those cats of hers."

"Kerry, do you dislike her so much that you want her to die?"

"No, of course not."

"Well, then, we've got to make friends with her. Because we've got to get her to quit working in the nurse's office at school. Kerry, in that book, Beth *dies* — before she's even out of her teens. And you know why? She catches something from people she's nursing."

Kerry looked half incredulous and half furious. "Have you gone completely crackers? You're talking about a character in a book, Lori! Not a real person. Not the girl next door. Not real life."

"Yeah, well, I just tossed it off like that, too, when all I knew was that those girls next door have almost the same names and personality traits as the ones in the book," I snapped. "Gee whiz, what an amusing coincidence, I thought.

But not anymore. This stuff goes much further than coincidence, and it's getting scary and dangerous and too close for comfort. Kerry, I think that book is some sort of weird premonition for the family next door."

She slapped her forehead in exasperation. "Lori, when are you going to start realizing that fiction is *fiction*? Made up? Imagined? Fantasy time? All straight out of the author's head?"

"I *do* realize that, except in this one case — "

"Are you forgetting the time you grabbed my arm in B. Dalton's bookstore and pointed out that tall, black-haired guy with the beady, black eyes? You thought he was Heathcliff come to life."

I felt my face turning red, but I managed a haughty toss of my head. "I did not. I said he *looked* like Heathcliff was supposed to have looked."

She snorted. "Liar."

"Well, that guy *was* thumbing through a copy of *Wuthering Heights*," I said.

"Or how about the time at the mall you were sure you saw Nancy Drew sitting by the fountain?"

"Well, that girl was blonde and she was with a tall, thin guy, a dumpy fat girl eating a candy bar, and an athletic-looking girl with short, dark hair and a tennis racket. Voilà: Nancy, her boyfriend Ned, and her best pals and cousins George and Bess."

"Yeah, and I'm — "

"Look, Kerry," I interrupted, "I bet most authors base their characters on real-life people. And those people at the mall just happened to be the Nancy Drew author's models."

"Lori, I think the first Nancy Drew mysteries were written like a hundred years ago. That would make the real-life Nancy model and her pals pretty ancient, or probably dead."

"Oh, yeah," I said very quietly, ducking my head.

"And the same would hold true if Louisa May Alcott based *Little Women* on real-life people," Kerry said. "Your problem is you just take books too seriously."

I rushed over and yanked the book away from her, flipping through it to a page I'd marked with a piece of paper. "Kerry, I may have thought those people at the mall and that guy in the bookstore looked and sort of acted like their respective book characters. But, like I said before, the Marches and the Marshes have much more in common than looks and personality traits. There's something really spooky going on . . . something cosmic. . . ."

Kerry disdainfully hummed the first few bars of the *Twilight Zone* theme.

Ignoring her, I found the page I wanted. "Look here — the father in the book: He's away in the military, too. Just like Captain Marsh. And he gets some strange disease. *And* the mother goes to nurse him back to health." I turned to another marked page. "Meanwhile, back at home, Beth gets really sick, a nasty little bug she's picked up from a local family *she* is nursing back to health. Oh, Kerry, there's even a domineering Aunt March who comes to stay with the girls while their mother is gone. Don't you remember?" I shivered at the weirdness of it all.

Kerry's green eyes were practically popping out of her head at me. "Do both the father and Beth die? I don't remember."

"Uh-uh. The father recovers and comes home. But Beth just gets weaker and weaker as the years go by, and finally she just — "

Kerry had slapped her hands over her ears. "You're talking about a book, not real life," she said again, but her voice was shaky this time.

I went over and pried her hands loose, then bent down so I could talk to her eye-to-eye. "Kerry, do you really want to chance it? What if I'm right and the book really is some sort of

52

eerie prediction? Do you really want to chance the possibility of having Bethanny's death hanging over your head for the rest of your life? When you could have prevented it?"

Kerry heaved a huge, defeated sigh. "What should we do?"

"Like I said, we've got to get her to quit the nurse's office. And we've got to promise each other that we will not divulge any of the *Little Women* coincidences to any of the Marshes — especially Bethanny."

Kerry gasped. "Why not? Seems to me that would be the easiest way to convince her that — "

"Absolutely not!" I cried, taking her by the shoulders and shaking her. "Kerry, wouldn't you just die if you knew your potential fate like Bethanny would if she read that book? She might go psycho on us or something. It's too big a risk."

"I see your point," Kerry said thoughtfully. "Okay, my lips are sealed about the book. At least in the dear girl's presence. But how are we going to get her out of that nurse's office?"

I went to my window and peered down, my eyes finding the Marshes' front door in the early-morning gloom. "Don't worry, I think I have a plan. After all, I stayed awake most of the night, worrying about this. I'm gonna aim straight for Bethanny's sympathetic, do-gooder heart. Now, I'll keep a lookout. You just be ready to leave for school the instant Bethanny walks out her front door."

"That's at least an hour away," Kerry groaned. "I'll see you then." She flopped back on my bed and closed her eyes.

When I muttered "There she is!" about 55 minutes later, however, Kerry sprang up and flew down the stairs and out the door with me.

Bethanny seemed very pleased to be walking to school with us, but she was also her usual annoyingly apologetic and rather retiring self. "Don't feel you have to include me in your conversation," she said, before we'd walked a half a block. "Just listening to people is fine with me. That is, unless there's something you don't want me to hear, in which case I can just walk several steps behind you guys, or cross the street, or maybe — "

"Bethanny, I have a problem I'd like your input on," I interrupted to shut her up.

"Oh, gee, oh, how can I help?" she babbled eagerly. "Oh, please, tell me what's wrong, because if I can help in any way. . . ."

She was *so* easy to set up!

I strove for a pathetic but authentic-sounding stutter of despair. "Well, the problem is I'm so far behind on my gossip column that the

". . . the . . . the f-f-faculty adviser of the newspaper is going to f-f-fire me unless I can get an assistant to help me," I lied. I even managed to make my eyes fill with tears, mainly by thinking about Bethanny dying.

"Oh, Lori, you mean all you need is an assistant?" Bethanny cried.

I nodded, wiping my eyes. "Just for a couple of hours after school each day." The same hours Bethanny did her stint in the nurse's office, to be exact.

Bethanny threw a puzzled glance in Kerry's direction.

Kerry cleared her throat. "I . . . uh . . . can't help Lori because I . . . uh . . . work for my mom every day after school."

Bethanny took my arm gently. "Lori, I'd be glad to help. I'll take the job as your assistant. That is, if you'll have me. I mean, I have no newspaper experience. Oh, dear . . . please, please don't feel you *have* to hire me. Certainly, I'll understand if you want someone with more — "

"I'll take you, I'll take you!" I interrupted, relieved.

Bethanny's face crinkled up with worry. "Of course, I'm going to have to give the nurse some notice before I can quit working in the nurse's office. Just a few days, maybe, until they can find someone to replace me."

"Oh, no, please, you can't!" I wailed. "Mrs. Caprice said I had to have an assistant starting *today* or . . ." I made the throat-slashing gesture.

Bethanny looked truly tortured: Who should she let down — me or the nurse? In the end, the nurse didn't stand a chance, thanks to plenty of additional snivelling and whining on my part.

As soon as we got to school, Kerry and I left Bethanny. I went to find Big Guy. If Bethanny and I were going to be working on the column for two hours every weekday afternoon, Big Guy and I would have to reschedule our Tuesday-Thursday tutorials. And our Monday afternoons at the mall. And our Friday afternoons at the Corvette Café. An ache of regret mixed with a twinge of annoyance surged through me. How I wished I'd never met Bethanny! "But remember," I muttered aloud, "this is a matter of life and death." And only temporary, I hoped. Just until Bethanny's nurse's-office position was filled by somebody else and a new position opened up that would appeal to her do-gooder instincts and sap her spare time. Say, in the library. Or in the gym. *Anywhere* that she wouldn't be around sick people.

Big Guy was not only furious, he was extremely suspicious. *"Every single day?"* he nearly shouted, slamming his locker closed. "Since when have you needed two hours a day to write that thing, let alone an assistant? Maybe I'll just happen to be walking past the newspaper office this afternoon around two-thirty. We'll just see if you're in there working with Bethanny Marsh!"

"It's Wednesday. You have to work at your mom's store."

"Okay, then I'll just happen to walk by the office *tomorrow*, okay? You can't fool me, Laigen. Bethanny Marsh, of all people! You can come up with a better story than that! Why don't you just tell the truth? Who is it that's really your so-called 'assistant'? Danny Farmer? Or ... uh ... that guy who always walks out of your English class with you?"

He was getting angrier and angrier, and finally I decided I'd have to do what I'd vowed the night before not to do: I'd have to tell him the whole Marsh Family/March Family story.

The warning bell rang.

I sighed. "Look, Big Guy, at lunch I'll tell you the whole truth, okay?"

He looked miserable, but his eyes gleamed a bit in triumph that he had succeeded in forcing me to come clean. I'm sure he was expecting a lunchtime confession that I had fallen madly in love with Rodney McCall, the little wimp who always followed me out of English, or some other equally ridiculous thing.

At lunch, we went off on our own to a quiet, tree-shaded corner of the student quad, and I recited the entire Marsh/March saga so far, from the similarity in the names/ages/personalities to dengue fever and the nurse's office. He just sat there, and I could tell he was struggling to keep his face expressionless. But his eyes were bulging out more and more by the second. When I finished, he just continued to stare at me, speechless.

"Well," I said, after a long silence, "go ahead. Call me insane, crackers, crazy, bonkers, schiz-y. Maybe I am."

Big Guy had once told me he'd read somewhere that if you could admit to possibly being one of those things, you more than likely weren't. Watching his face, I could tell he was remembering that.

"I don't think *you* are crazy," he finally said. "But I think this whole theory of yours is just totally bizarr-o. That's my first reaction. My second reaction is I'm relieved. Really relieved. I mean, nobody — not even you, with your wild, literary imagination — would come up with a story like that just to cover up that she's cheating."

I opened my book bag and took out my well-worn copy of *Little Women*. "Look, the only way you're going to believe me is by reading this." I thrust it into his hands.

He took one look at it and thrust it right back at me, almost violently. "I'm not reading *that*." He took a fast look around to see if anyone had caught him even touching the thing. It was as if I'd handed him a book like *Embroidery For All Your Frilly Little Things* or something.

"Well, if you're not going to read it," I snapped, "then at least humor me on this thing, will you? Just bear with me for a couple of weeks, okay? Because I'm not taking any chances."

He sighed. "Okay. I mean, what you're doing may be totally bizarr-o, but it's also probably harmless."

Still, he looked sort of skeptical. My head began to throb, and I was tempted to say "You're right. This is ridiculous. Let's both just forget the whole thing." But before I could get my mouth open, an image of Bethanny flickered across my mind, and I was haunted by those kind, caring, trusting eyes. There were so few people like her left in the world . . . suddenly, more than ever, I felt obligated, even *honored* to do everything in my power to make sure we didn't lose her.

Chapter 5

What blonde beach betty was recently seen at Sluggo's, fingers intertwined with those of an already-taken basketball guard?

"Hmm," I said, copying the tip into my notebook, "Alicia Jeffreys usually only goes for surfer types. I wonder why she's suddenly hot for Bramer Badham?"

"Are you going to run that tip?" Bethanny asked. It was already three-thirty on the first day she went to work as my assistant. She'd sat through the usual Wednesday-afternoon newspaper staff meeting with me, smiling sweetly and seemingly unaware that everyone was whispering comments like "She and Joanne Marsh are *sisters*? Nah!" Now we were all alone in the newspaper office. The Bramer Badham/Alicia Jeffreys tip was the first I'd picked up.

"No, I'm not going to run it like it is," I said absently, continuing to write. "I hate the term *beach betty*. It's sexist, surfer lingo. Let's make it . . . *beachy blonde*. That's not so bad."

"And that's the only change you're going to make?" Bethanny's voice quavered. I finally looked up at her. To my surprise, her eyes were filled with tears!

"What's wrong, Bethanny?"

"Printing that would just be so . . . so . . . *cruel*!"

My mouth dropped open. This particular tip was pretty tame, as tips go. "What do you mean by that?"

"Well, can you imagine how hurt and rejected Veronica Campbell is going to feel when she reads it? I've heard she's been Bramer's girlfriend for two years. It's just so mean, Lori."

"It's not mean, Bethanny, it's gossip! It's my job!" I went on copying the tip into my English notebook, which is where I always wrote the first draft of my column.

Bethanny reached over and grabbed the hand that was writing. "Oh, Lori, please don't run it! Or at least not before one of us talks to Bramer. That way, the item won't be such a blow to poor Veronica."

"Talk to Bramer about what?"

"Well, one of us should let him know that it's pretty common knowledge that he's secretly seeing Alicia. We should encourage him to have a long, honest talk with Veronica. Get everything out in the open."

"Do I look like Ann Landers?" I asked. I continued with my writing. "Forget it, Bethanny. It's going in as is. And in the next issue."

She grabbed my hand again. "Then at least disguise the people more. *Please?* Please, Lori? Then maybe Veronica will just be *suspicious* — not sure — that it's Bramer we're talking about. That'll lead to a confrontation between the two, I hope, which will clear the air. And I'll feel so good about it, Lori! I'll feel like we've really helped them."

I sighed. "How do you suggest we disguise the item more?"

She closed her eyes tightly and was silent for a minute. " 'What blonde was seen holding hands with what already-taken athlete at what local restaurant?' " she finally suggested.

I slapped my forehead in exasperation. "Oh, terrific. That'll narrow the field down to about 94 already-taken athletes and 136 possible blondes. Oh . . . and, say, 7,002 restaurants in the Greater San Diego area."

"Okay . . . I get your point," Bethanny said,

giggling. "Let's make it . . . 'at what *Mission Hills* restaurant.' "

"Fine! Narrows the possible restaurants down to about 36, not including the fast-food places," I snapped.

We went back and forth like that for another twenty minutes. Finally, I just threw up my hands. "All right, Bethanny, all right already! Let's just go on to the next tip, okay?" I crossed out the Bramer/Alicia tip in my notebook, but slipped the original tip slip into my pocket.

Bethanny's face lit up with a sweetly triumphant but grateful smile. She was unaware, of course, that I planned to stick the thing back in the column — beachy blonde/basketball guard language intact — as soon as I got home and was alone at my desk in my room.

I unfolded the next tip:

It seems Ryan Janeway is in the habit of retrieving the morning newspaper in his underwear. A group of cheerleaders, driving past the Janeway house on their way to a before-school breakfast meeting at Denny's restaurant, got an eyeful on Friday morning. And guess what? Ryan's face is not the only part of his body that blushes!

I leaned back in my chair and howled with laughter. Ryan Janeway was such an arrogant, preppie, proper snob. And he'd been caught in his front yard in his skivs! Oh, this was *rich*!

Bethanny picked up the slip of paper and gasped as she read it. A little warning bell pinged in my head. I tried to ignore it as I began to copy the tip into my notebook. But within seconds, Bethanny's hand was on top of mine, stopping it.

"Oh, Lori, we can't run this tip! It'll just rekindle the horrible embarrassment Ryan must have felt that morning. Imagine how it would feel to have the *whole school* — not just a çarful of cheerleaders — ridiculing you, laughing at you!"

"It serves him right!" I said. "Look, Bethanny, anybody who goes out in public in his underwear has to recognize the danger and accept the consequences."

"At least say he was wearing his swim trunks," Bethanny begged. "He probably was."

"At six-thirty in the morning? On a school day? In January? Forget it!"

"Well, still, give him the benefit of the doubt. Those girls can't be sure he wasn't wearing swim trunks. I mean, swim trunks and underwear look a lot alike."

I smiled. "Only if the underwear are boxer

shorts. Jockey shorts look nothing like swim trunks."

She blushed furiously. I'd forgotten she had no brothers and wasn't savvy to male underwear styles. Still, what a prude!

Seeing her discomfort, I couldn't help needling her a bit. All this arguing was getting on my nerves. "Wait a minute, Bethanny," I said, trying to keep a straight face. "You've got a point. It could have been swim trunks after all. So here's what I want you to do, Assistant. Tomorrow, you're to ask Ryan Janeway whether he wears boxers or jockeys. It's the only way we'll be able to confirm this."

Now her face turned absolutely scarlet and I was sure she was about to surrender. Wrong.

"Well . . . I'll just *die* when I ask him. But I did take this job, after all. And if checking on facts like that is part of the job, well . . . then I'll just have to take a deep breath and do it!"

I bit back a groan of despair. "Forget it, Bethanny. I changed my mind. It's not necessary to ask him."

Relief flooded her face. "Then you're not going to run the item?"

"Tell you what. I'll run it, but I won't use his name. I'll say 'It seems a certain junior who lives on Delatour Street blah blah blah.' " Was

I crafty or what? The Janeways were the only people who lived on Delatour Street, but Bethanny wouldn't know that.

"Oh, no, Lori, that won't work. The Janeways are the only family that lives on Delatour Street."

This time, I couldn't stifle a groan. "Now, how did you know that? You guys have been in Mission Hills only a couple of weeks, and Delatour's way over by Presidio Park."

She smiled gently. "Mother and I have done a lot of collecting for the March of Dimes over in that area."

We stared at each other for a long minute, each waiting for the other to give in.

"I have an idea," she finally said. "Use the item, but instead of giving Ryan's name, say 'a junior from western Mission Hills.' "

She saw that I was about to have an exasperation explosion.

"Or at least say that he looked *attractive* in his underwear," she said hurriedly. "Handsome, hunky, something. That would take some of the sting out of the humiliation."

When I got home an hour later, I had a raging headache, a notebook page full of crossed-out tips, and an urge to murder Bethanny.

That last thought at least allowed me to crack

a half smile at myself in the medicine cabinet mirror as I took an aspirin. "That's great, Laigen. You want to murder her when you're doing this whole thing to keep her from dying."

Our column sessions on Thursday and Friday were almost exact reruns of Wednesday, except that each day we battled over a whole new crop of tips . . . or "mean tips," as Bethanny referred to them. The only way I managed to keep my sanity was to go home each afternoon after our session and ruthlessly cut the tips she had begged to have included — stuff she herself had submitted about people doing volunteer work or being particularly cheerful or helpful. Then I'd reinsert the good dirt she had campaigned so vigorously against.

On Friday night, when Big Guy, Kerry, Kerry's off-and-on boyfriend Dieter, and I were just sitting around watching TV at my house, I brought down a pageful of Bethanny's cloying tips both for laughs and for verification that I was doing the right thing.

Kerry read it first. "Yawn," she said, passing it on to Big Guy.

"Snore," he said, passing it on to Dieter.

"Bleaghh!" Dieter said, making the finger-down-the-throat gesture.

* * *

The following Tuesday, my column came out as catty, witty, and juicy as ever.

Bethanny arrived for our usual after-school session white-faced and with trembling lips. "Oh, Lori, did you see what happened to our column?"

I nodded sadly. "The editor — Katie Tarantino — did it. I'm sorry, Bethanny, but I have to submit *all* the gossip tips we get — even the ones we reject — to Katie with my final draft," I lied blithely. "She has final say on what goes in and what doesn't." I knew sweet little Bethanny would never have the guts to confront Katie about this.

Bethanny took a deep breath. "Well, then, I guess what we'll have to do in the future is not submit *all* of the tips we get to Katie. We'll just give her the ones that we don't mind seeing in print."

I gasped and put my hand to my throat in mock horror. "Are you suggesting we *lie*, Bethanny?"

She blushed and hung her head. "Sometimes a little white lie is necessary to save a person's feelings. In this case, *a lot* of peoples' feelings."

Inward groan time. How was I going to get out of *this* one?

That night, I tossed and turned over the

problem. It seemed like the only choices I had were to let Bethanny turn my column into a high school version of *Mister Rogers' Neighborhood* or to fire her and run the risk that she might take her old nurse's-office job back. I woke up at dawn, exhausted, having come to no solution. I was just lying there, fretting, when I heard a soft voice below.

" 'Bye-bye, Muffin! 'Bye, Snowball, Teddy, and Fluffy! Be good. See you this afternoon."

The voice was Bethanny's. The dumb names? Her cats'.

I got up and went to the window, curious. It was barely light. The sun hadn't yet risen. But I could clearly see Bethanny. And she was carrying her schoolbooks.

I opened the window. "Bethanny!" I hissed in a stage whisper. "Why are you going to school so early?"

She glanced up at me, startled. "Oh, Lori! Hi! Oh, dear, did I wake you up? Oh, I am *so* sorry. Me and my big mouth! I am so sorry — "

"I was already awake." I cut her off. "How come you're leaving so early?"

"I always leave this early. Or, I have since I started working with you. I mean, I have nurse's-office duty in the mornings now, before school. They let me switch my hours. And I like to get there a little early to make sure everything's clean and neat before any students come in."

I grabbed my head and groaned. "No! No! No!"

Bethanny was staring up at me, eyes wide with concern. "Are you sick, Lori? Maybe you ought to come to the nurse's office before school. I can take your temperature and — "

"I'm fine!" I said, slamming the window closed. She waved good-bye. I just stood there at the window, watching. Bethanny disappeared into the darkness. And so did my plan to keep her away from sickies.

When Kerry came to pick me up for school an hour and a half later, I was on the verge of tears. "That little sneak has been working in the nurse's office in the *mornings*," I burst out.

"Look, you can't really call her a sneak," Kerry said. "After all, she doesn't know we're trying to keep her out of the nurse's office, remember?"

"Well, what do we do now?" I wailed.

"Nothing," Kerry said. "We did what we could, and it didn't work. So let's just forget the whole thing."

I stamped my foot. "No! I can't forget it! Listen, last night, when I was tossing and turning, I came up with yet another weirdly eerie parallel between the Marshes and the Marches. One that didn't register before."

Kerry sighed. "Now what?"

"Before Mrs. Marsh left for Kuwait, she did a lot of volunteer work, just like Mrs. March did."

"Lori, most of the Mission Hills moms who don't have jobs do volunteer work, and you know it."

I shrugged into my denim jacket then whirled around to face Kerry. "Are you my best friend or not? If you are, you'll help me come up with a new plan to get Bethanny out of that office if for no other reason than you know it will make me happy! I told you, Kerry, I'm not taking any chances!"

"But, Lori, I just feel so bad about — "

"Look, don't you think I feel guilty rotten about all this, too? About the lies we've had to tell her? About the other crummy ways we've manipulated her?"

"*You've* manipulated her," Kerry corrected.

I ignored her. "But I'll tell you, I'd much rather deal with guilt than deal with grief. All I have to do is picture it: Bethanny lying in a satin-lined coffin, six million people she's been nice to crowding into the church, poor little Amanda weeping in the front pew — " I caught my breath in a sob.

"All right, already," Kerry said gruffly.

I gathered my books. "Now think about it all day. We've got to put a new plan into action tomorrow morning at the very latest."

A horn tooted. Kerry went to the window. "Oh, it's just one of Megan's Morons. I've never seen this one before."

I joined Kerry at the window. A Rabbit convertible had pulled into the Marshes' driveway. A good-looking blond guy jumped out. He headed for the Marshes' front door, but Megan came out and met him halfway, skipping down the front steps in a red corduroy miniskirt.

"Erik, hi!" she called, taking his hand. "I was just sitting in there, worrying about how I was going to get to school."

Kerry groaned. "Does she use the same lines every single day or what?"

"You're the only guy who ever worries about me, and I appreciate it so, so much!" Megan and Kerry trilled together. Megan stood on her tiptoes and kissed the guy's cheek.

"Have you noticed that she's the only person in the entire Marsh family to have a southern accent?" I asked. "And it's not a very good one, either."

We watched the couple head for the Rabbit, swinging hands. The guy was so busy staring at Megan that he tripped over an ornamental rock in the front yard. Kerry and I quietly cracked up.

The Marshes' front door opened again, and Aunt Marsh came out and stood on the porch, arms folded across her chest. She looked massive in an olive-green housecoat and fuzzy gray slippers. "You kids go directly to school, you hear?" she hollered. She watched them drive off, then went back into the house, the screen door banging behind her.

Within a minute, a red Honda Accord pulled into the Marshes' driveway. "Here comes another one," I said, "right on schedule. He doesn't know it, but he was to serve only as a back-up ride, should Megan's preferred driver — the guy in the Rabbit — fail to show."

Kerry clicked her tongue. "She's not as dumb as she acts. But she sure is cutting it close. What if the guys had shown up at the same time? What does she do in that case?"

"Hasn't happened yet," I said. "I'm sure she schedules them carefully. But you're right. Today was really a close call. Notice how she didn't dare even wait for the Rabbit guy to get to the front door. She hustled him right off to the car. And just in time. They were barely around the corner when this one showed up."

The Honda guy went to the Marshes' front

door. After a minute, he returned to his car, dragging his feet with disappointment.

Aunt Marsh came out to the porch again. "You go directly to school, do you hear?" she hollered after the poor kid, as Kerry and I mouthed the words along with her.

I giggled. "Let's make a lot of noise when we leave today, okay? Maybe Aunt Marsh will come out and yell that at us, too. Want to stake some money on it?"

But Kerry was still bristling about Megan and her devious ways. "You know what I want to do as soon as I get my driver's license?" she asked. "I'm gonna drive my mom's car over here some morning, wait till the first guy's car is parked in the Marshes' driveway and then, purely by accident, of course, I'm gonna park right behind it, blocking the driveway until the second guy shows up. Sabotage! I'd just love to see Megan squirm, racking her brain desperately for new lines, when she has to — "

I grabbed Kerry's arms. "That's *it*, Ker! You've found the solution to the Bethanny-nurse's office dilemma!"

"I did? What? What'd I say?"

"Sabotage. Let me put it another way. Since we couldn't get Bethanny to quit the nurse's office, . . . " my tone was grim but resolute, ". . . well, then, we'll just have to get her *fired*."

Chapter 6

On a Friday night a week and a half later, Kerry and I found ourselves at the Marshes', attending a slumber party in celebration of Bethanny's fifteenth birthday.

"You'd think at fifteen Bethanny would be old enough to have a *real* party," Kerry had grumbled. "You know, with *boys*."

"Give her a few years," I'd said. "She's still so shy and naive."

At eleven o'clock, Bethanny, Kerry, Megan, Amanda, and I were gathered in front of a roaring fire in the Marshes' family room. Wearing our nightgowns, we were sharing two huge bowls of popcorn, and trading terrifying "true" tales, such as the one about the babysitter who keeps getting threatening phone calls and finally learns that the guy is calling from a bedroom *upstairs*.

Suddenly, the front door burst open, and Bethanny shrieked in fear. But it was only Joanne, home from a date. She laughed. "Bloody bones and butcher knives and all that baloney."

"Who did you go out with?" I asked her politely.

"Brian," she said, which was about as helpful as asking a directory assistance operator in Los Angeles for the phone number of "John Smith." I mean, I knew eleven Brians in the freshman class alone. But Joanne declined to elaborate.

"Come and join us, Joanne," Bethanny said.

"No, thanks. I'm almost at the end of a juicy novel and I have to finish it," she said.

"That's all you ever do around here," Amanda grumbled. "Read."

"Just like Jo!" I mouthed at Kerry.

"Anyway, slumber parties are a waste of time," Joanne said. "All they do is put you behind schedule, since you have to spend the whole next day sleeping." She ran up the stairs, two at a time.

I sighed. "That's exactly what Big Guy said."

"Who's Big Guy?" Amanda asked.

"B.G. Grimes. My boyfriend."

Megan's huge blue eyes gleamed with predatory interest. "You have a boyfriend?"

"Oh, give it a rest, Megan," Amanda

snapped. "Don't you have enough boyfriends as it is?"

Megan sighed. "So many men, so little time."

"How original," Kerry said, aiming an obvious look at the front of Megan's nightshirt, which featured that same slogan. Kerry then tried to catch my eyes, for about the 77th time that evening. This was the first occasion — at least officially — that she was in Megan's presence, and Kerry wasn't doing a very good job of hiding her lack of enthusiasm for the girl. Whenever she wasn't shooting me incredulous looks, she was rolling her eyes or shaking her head in wonder at the things Megan said.

They'd sort of gotten off on the wrong foot anyway. The first thing Kerry had said, with wide, innocent eyes, upon being introduced to Megan was, "You're Joanne and Bethanny's *sister*? Why, I thought you were a cousin from Alabama or something. I mean, I overheard you talking to a boy in your yard when I was over at Lori's one day, and I'm sure I remember your having a southern accent."

Megan, who wasn't using her southern accent that night — after all, there were only us *girls* around — had shot Kerry a look of pure daggers. "Perhaps your ears need cleaning," she'd said sweetly.

Now Megan grabbed a pillow from the couch

and hugged it. "Anyway, tell us all about your boyfriend, Lori," she said.

I sighed. "He may be my *ex*-boyfriend. We had a fight this afternoon."

Bethanny gasped. "Oh, no, Lori! Are you okay? What did you fight about? Do you want to talk about it?"

We had fought about her, actually, but I refrained from saying so. Otherwise, Bethanny would probably apologize to me for a solid month. "It was no big deal," I said. "And I'd rather not talk about it here, Bethanny, and spoil your party."

"Oh, I'm sorry!" she cried. "Oh, I'm so sorry for being so nosy! Will you forgive me for — ?"

I tuned her out as the endless string of apologies continued. I turned my thoughts to Big Guy. Did we have any future?

He had been furious when I told him I would be attending Bethanny's all-girl slumber party, since he and I had been spending every Friday and Saturday night together.

"Bethanny Marsh again!" he had practically shouted into the phone. "Don't you spend enough time with her as it is? You're with her for two solid hours every single day after school!"

I'd tried to keep my voice calm, reasonable. "Look, Big Guy, the more time I can spend with her the better, until I can once and for all get her out of that nurse's office. This way I can make sure that, outside of the nurse's office, at least, she's not associating with anybody contagious. By the way, is it true that Raymond Kraft has mono or was that just a rumor? He sits next to Bethanny in — "

"That stupid book again!" he interrupted, and this time he really was shouting. "I think you ought to see a shrink, Laigen, and right away — "

"Don't you dare judge my mental health, B.G. Grimes, until you've read the book!" I shouted back. "I don't want to hear another word about this from you until you do!"

He slammed the phone down, but not before I'd shrieked "Read the book!" two more times.

I hadn't even had the chance to tell him that I would no longer be spending afternoons with Bethanny. I had fired her that very afternoon. I would have done so sooner — i.e., the day I found out she was still working in the nurse's office — except that I was afraid she'd get suspicious that those two activities were somehow linked. But the fact of the matter was, Bethanny was the least suspicious of all the people I'd ever met in my entire life, and that included babies.

"Look, Bethanny, you can't be my assistant

anymore because Mrs. Caprice is making us cut back on staff," is how she got the ax. It was a perfectly ridiculous excuse on my part, since nobody was getting a salary so there was no reason in the world to cut back on staff. If I were Bethanny, I would have demanded — my voice thick with suspicion — to know why, if the staff was being cut, my own sister Joanne wasn't also being let go due to her lack of seniority.

But I'm not Bethanny. And like I said, that girl didn't have a suspicious bone in her body. She accepted the story with her usual compassion and a couple of apologies along the lines of, "I'm sorry I put you in the position of having to let me go, Lori. I know that's a real tough thing to do."

"Oh, Bethie, don't cry!"

Amanda's voice jolted me from my memories. Megan had her arms around Bethanny, who was crying on her shoulder. Amanda was patting Bethanny's arm. Kerry was aiming a this-is-all-your-fault glare at me. I tuned back into the conversation.

"And . . . and . . . Mrs. McSween, the nurse, said she'll have to fire me if it happens again," Bethanny sobbed.

At the sight of her tears, my heart flopped over with anguish, yet simultaneously soared with hope, if that's possible. "Bethanny, I'm sorry, I was reliving my fight with Big Guy and didn't hear what you were talking about," I said quickly. "Will someone fill me in?"

"Twice this week, poor Bethanny's been accused of being 'derelict in her nurse's-office duties,' quote unquote," Amanda said indignantly.

"On Tuesday afternoon, a couple of angry mothers called the principal and said that their sick kids had gone to the nurse's office before school that morning and found the door locked," Megan continued.

Bethanny blew her nose. "Before school — that's when I'm supposed to be on duty," she said.

"Well, you *were*," Amanda said. "You haven't missed a single day. You must have just forgotten to unlock the door once you got inside." She turned to me. "These mothers said their kids knocked and knocked but got no answer. We figure Bethanny just didn't hear them because she was back in the storage room or vacuuming the carpet or something."

Actually, the principal had broached those same lame possibilities when Angry Mother #1 had called him. I ought to know. By the time Mother #2 phoned in he had changed his tune. "The girl who was supposed to be on duty must have been out on the student quad, yakking with her friends," he'd told a muffled, middle-aged Kerry.

Bethanny sniffled. "I just felt so bad when the nurse yelled at me about those poor kids. They were probably so weak and nauseated and feverish. One of the mothers told the principal her son nearly fainted from the exertion of knocking on the door for so long. She said he finally just staggered home. To think that I was probably all warm and cozy on the other side of the door . . . without a care in the world." She sobbed out the last word.

"And then yesterday morning, Thursday, when the nurse got to the office there was glass all over the floor," Amanda explained to me, putting an arm around Bethanny's shoulders.

"It was the . . . the big glass jar we keep tongue depressors in," Bethanny said. "And I just can't understand it. I mean, it was still sitting where it always sits when I left the office at eight. That's when I have to leave for home-room. So it must have happened between eight and eight-twenty, when Mrs. McSween gets there. That's when her bus arrives at school. There must have been a small earthquake or something."

Good old Bethanny. She'd blame Mother Nature, but it never occurred to her to blame a real person.

"But the nurse yelled at Bethanny *again*," Megan informed me.

"She thinks Bethanny broke the jar and was just too lazy to clean it up," Amanda said. "Our Bethanny being accused of leaving a mess! It's the dumbest thing I've ever heard."

Bethanny cringed at the memory, then dabbed at her eyes with a tissue. "Mrs. McSween said by breaking the jar and leaving it — which I didn't — I put hundreds of students at risk of serious injury."

I snorted. "Oh, come on. McSween's so melodramatic she ought to switch jobs with the drama teacher."

Amanda was bouncing up and down on the couch indignantly. "Well, I think some low-life, some Neanderthal went in there and vandalized the place just for kicks."

Bethanny shook her head. "Oh, no, honey. Nobody would do such — "

"Yes, they would!" Amanda said.

"Amanda, really, I don't believe that. I mean, everybody has to be in their homerooms between eight and eight-thirty." Suddenly, Bethanny's voice broke, and she sobbed pitifully. Kerry shot me another you're-responsible glare. I felt tears stinging behind my own eyes, but I pressed my lips together stubbornly and returned a matter-of-life-and-death/only-for-her-own-good look.

"Bethie, look," Amanda said. "The locked-door thing was probably a simple mistake on your part that won't happen again. As for the tongue-depressor jar, believe whatever you want. Maybe it *was* just an earthquake or something — " She rolled her eyes. "But whatever or whoever did it, it could happen again. And you obviously don't want that because McSween will fire you. So the solution is simple. You've got to stay in the nurse's office an extra twenty minutes until the nurse gets there at eight-twenty. It's as simple as that."

No, no, no, don't, Bethany! I pleaded silently. *Reject Amanda's idea!* That twenty-minute period had been tailor-made for sabotage. I'd already cooked up a few other schemes for the time slot should the angry mothers and tongue-depressor jar not do the trick.

Bethanny's hand flew to her mouth. "I can't skip homeroom, Amanda. Homeroom is mandatory."

"Didn't you tell me your homeroom teacher is really nice?" Megan piped up. "Mr. . . . uh . . . Lang?"

"Mr. Lane," Bethanny said.

Amanda started bouncing again. "So you could explain the problem to him . . . ask him if it will be all right to be a few minutes late every day. He'd understand."

Kerry cleared her throat. "Right. After all, what would you be missing in homeroom? All they ever do there is take roll and read the bulletin. You could leave the nurse's office at eight-twenty, and that would still give you ten minutes to get to homeroom and say 'I'm here.'"

I shot Kerry a look of loathing. Whose side are you on, you traitor? I thought.

Bethanny was nodding thoughtfully. "I think I can convince Mr. Lane. After all, I'd be late only because I'm performing a service for the school, not because I overslept or something." Suddenly, a warm, happy smile broke over her face and she beamed at each of us in turn. "Thanks for helping me! I'll go talk to Mr. Lane first thing Monday morning!"

"Okay, girls, hit the hay! Get the lead out and hit the hay!"

All five of us jumped ten feet. Aunt Marsh was standing at the bottom of the stairs, arms crossed over her chest. She headed for us, clapping her hands. "Come on, now, get in those sleeping bags on the double!"

Bethanny just about leaped into hers.

"But Aunt Marsh, this is a slumber party," Amanda whined. "We're supposed to stay up all night. It's not even midnight."

"A *what* party? If it's a slumber party then you're gonna slumber, got it?" Aunt Marsh shook her finger at Amanda and then at Megan. "You will not stay up all night. I've never heard of a more ridiculous thing. Now hit those sacks, pronto!"

Amanda crossed her arms, and set her face, and suddenly looked a lot like Aunt Marsh. "No. Mom lets us have a slumber party practically every other month."

"Any Marsh girl who is not in her sleeping bag within thirty seconds, and asleep within ten minutes, will make up for it tomorrow night, Saturday night, by going to bed at seven!" Aunt Marsh thundered. "That means no dates!"

Megan uttered a little shriek and headed for her sleeping bag.

"Oh, darn!" Amanda said sarcastically. "No dates. What a shame." She hadn't yet started going out with guys.

"And no TV!" Aunt Marsh bellowed.

Amanda was in her sleeping bag in a flash. The rest of us, the non-Marshes, meekly slid into our own bags. What else was there to do?

Aunt Marsh settled herself on the couch,

keeping watch. Soon, I heard Bethanny and Amanda's breathing get slow, deep, regular. The fire crackled a bit, its final warning that it was about to die. The grandfather clock's ticking got louder. And I was sort of glad Aunt Marsh had ordered us to bed. Finally, I could cry quietly into my pillow. Not just because I'd once again probably failed to get Bethanny out of the nurse's office. Big Guy kept swimming into my mind, too. An angry Big Guy.

Was this thing with Bethanny going to ruin — or had it *already* ruined — my relationship with the most wonderful guy I had ever known, the only boyfriend I had ever had? The grandfather clock ticked "Could be, could be, could be."

Chapter 7

When I woke up sunshine was slanting through the navy-blue Levelor blinds in the Marshes' family room. The smell of perking coffee and frying bacon wafted through the room. I found myself feeling stiff from the lack of a mattress but full of renewed hope. At least as far as Bethanny was concerned. There just had to be another way to get the nurse to fire her, and I was determined to find it.

Stretching, I stepped over two unidentifiable sleeping-bag-ensconced girls, burrowed worms, and sniffed my way to the kitchen.

"Morning!" a radiant Bethanny sang out as I stepped into the sun-splashed kitchen. "Isn't it a glorious morning?"

I smiled and joined Kerry at the kitchen table. Her eyelids were heavy, and her perm was smashed flat on one side. She was not a morning person.

Bethanny was at the stove, tending bacon with tongs in one hand, and flipping a pancake with the other. Within a minute, she was setting steaming plates in front of us. I'm not much of a breakfast eater, but that morning I dug in hungrily, mainly because pancakes and bacon were such a novel treat. Neither of those foods had darkened the doorway of my own home for at least ten years, since the day my father the doctor had begun to take a more "holistic" approach to medicine. Pancakes were off-limits because we weren't allowed to eat sugar before noon in his presence, and bacon had been expelled because of its "fat content and cancer-causing nitrates."

I ate six pieces at the Marshes, washing it down with apple juice. As I did, I watched Bethanny bustle around the kitchen. She was wearing one of the white, frilly blouses she favored under a delicately flowered-and-ruffled apron. Her long, reddish-brown hair was tied back with a black velvet ribbon. She looked very pretty and positively Victorian. So did the kitchen, for that matter, except for the presence of a dishwasher. Mrs. Marsh was obviously into antiques.

"Hey, Bethanny," I said, wiping my greasy

fingers on a blue gingham napkin, "tell us more about what you do in the nurse's office every day."

Kerry shot me a grumpy, warning look.

I ignored it and my own guilty feelings. "Like, how do you spend a typical hour in there?"

Bethanny chattered happily about taking temperatures, cleaning wounds with antiseptic, cuffing people to get their blood pressure readings. None of it sounded very promising in terms of troublemaking potential.

She went to the sink and rinsed her hands.

"And do you wash your hands after a sick person has been in?" I asked with utmost casualness, pretending to be mostly concerned with cutting my pancakes.

"Oh, sure, if I have time," Bethanny said, pouring more pancake batter into the frying pan. "Mrs. McSween says it's really important. In fact, she reminds me a lot: 'Wash your hands, wash your hands!' "

It was just a very slight imitation of the nurse — not really mean at all — but the instant Bethanny realized she had done it, she gasped with dismay and her hand flew to her mouth.

Kerry burst out laughing. "It's okay to mimic

people, Bethanny. I mean, it's not like she's here to hear you."

"Bethanny, you really shouldn't touch your nose and mouth as much as you do," I said, trying to keep the fretfulness out of my tone. "Especially since you work in the nurse's office. My dad says that's how most people get sick. They touch something with germs on it and then they touch their nose or mouth, transferring the germs."

Bethanny's hand flew to her mouth again. "Oh, I'm sorry, I should know that." She realized where her hand was. "Oh! How stupid of me!" She laughed nervously. "I'm sorry . . . I'm sorry I'm being so — "

"If you can't keep your hands away from your face, then it's absolutely essential that you wash your hands a lot," I cut in wearily. "So what else do you do in the nurse's office, Bethanny?"

"Well, there's some paperwork. The nurse fills out the admit slips that allow sick or hurt people to get back into class. Or get out of it. But we assistants are responsible for filling out the 'summary slips.' "

My ears pricked up hopefully. "What are those?" I asked, faking a yawn.

"We fill out one for each student who comes

in. You know, name of student, what the symptoms were, what the nurse's diagnosis was, if any, what treatment she prescribed, if any. Mrs. McSween says I do a very neat and thorough job. I'm the only one who types mine. The nurse is so impressed with the way I do it that she doesn't even check mine like she does the other girls'." Bethanny hung her head, embarrassed to be relating praise about herself.

"That's fab, Bethanny, real fab," Kerry said.

Bethanny beamed at her, missing the sarcasm.

"If the nurse doesn't read your summary slips, who does?" I asked, busily pouring syrup.

"Oh, the principal," Bethanny said. "And somebody at the school district office. Apparently, it's some sort of system for keeping track of how much work the nurse is doing. That's why she's grateful that I'm so thorough in my reports."

"But why are they keeping tabs on the nurse?" I asked, trying to hide my excitement.

"Because the school board wants to do some budget-cutting, and they're thinking of cutting the Nurses' Services Program," Bethanny said. "Mrs. McSween feels the summary slips prove just how valuable she is."

I slapped the table. "Oh, I know what slips you're talking about. I saw them in the nurse's office one day when I went to get a bandage for a blister. They're stored on a clipboard that's hanging on the wall behind McSween's desk, right?"

Bethanny piled more pancakes on my plate. "No. Those are the admit slips. We keep the summary slips in a box on the shelf that's right next to the first bed."

"And the principal looks at the slips every day?" I asked.

"Oh, no. Just once a week. Mrs. McSween almost always asks me to drop them off at his office sometime on Friday. I usually just carry them with me from class to class and drop them off right after lunch, since the administration office is right next to the gym, and I have P.E. fifth period."

My little tape recorder of a brain quietly clicked off.

A half-hour later, Kerry and I were standing on the Marshes' driveway, waiting for her mom to pick her up.

"The summary slips," I whispered. "That's it!"

Kerry shook her head so violently that her long, silver earrings slapped her jaw. "Are you crazy, or do you just have an IQ of ten?" she whispered back. "You can't steal those summary slips. Not after you asked her a million questions about them! She'd know in a second who did it!"

"Kerry, haven't you gotten the general idea yet? Bethanny thought an earthquake caused the tongue-depressor jar to fall on the floor, even though the 1,700 other glass jars in there didn't move a quarter of an inch. That girl is incapable of being suspicious."

"Well, her sisters aren't," Kerry snapped. "Especially Amanda."

"They weren't in the kitchen when we were talking about the summary slips. Anyway, cool it. I'm not going to steal them. That would be too obvious. McSween would certainly notice if there were no slips to give to Bethanny to take to the principal's office."

Kerry sighed. "Then what are you going to do with them?"

"What are *we* going to do with them? Let me think on it." I laughed softly and shook my head. "Knowing Bethanny and her bleeding heart, I bet she makes a simple sore throat sound like scarlet fever or something."

When I slipped through the hedges from the Marshes' yard to ours, I was both astonished and delighted to find Big Guy sitting on our front steps, reading a book. But I approached him warily. Was this good-bye? Was I about

94

to hear a farewell speech? Knowing Big Guy's methodical, mathematical mind, something along those lines would be just like him. Tie up all the loose ends. Make X minus Y equal Y minus X. Or whatever the correct equation is when two people break up.

But when he looked up at me, his eyes were filled with don't-be-mad. Silently he closed the book he had been reading and handed it to me. The title was *Escape from Omega II*. The thing pictured on the cover had a head that looked like it might have belonged to E.T.'s evil twin brother.

I thrust the book back at him. What a weird token of peace! "I hate sci-fi, and you know it," I said.

"Just read the first page," he said. "Even the first paragraph. *Please?*"

I sighed and opened the book to the first page. *"Christmas won't be Christmas without any presents,"* grumbled Jo, lying on the rug.

Laughing, I slipped the *Omega II* cover off the book. Sure enough, it was my copy of *Little Women*. "How did you get this?" I asked.

He ducked his head, embarrassed. "I came over early this morning and asked your mom if I could borrow it. Luckily, your brother wasn't up yet. I can just imagine the rumors that would spread if people knew I was reading *Little Women* by choice."

I smiled at him, delighted. "It won't make the school gossip column, I promise you. I know the columnist. She can be bribed." I sat down next to him. "Thanks for deciding to read it. I know it's not your type of thing."

He leaned over and kissed me very gently. "It's just not worth fighting over. I did a lot of thinking last night and decided that if this thing means so much to you, if you're getting so freaked out about it that it's affecting both of our lives, the least I can do is read the book so I can understand what you're talking about — ".

I squeezed his hand. "Thanks!"

" — even though I think what you're talking about is ridiculous," he added, his blue eyes twinkling.

I slapped him lightly with the book, then carefully put the sci-fi cover back on it. "How far have you read?"

"Not very. But far enough to see that Beth-anny is almost too sweet to stomach."

A thrill of satisfaction shot through me. "You mean Beth. Beth is the book character; Beth-anny is the girl next door," I said sweetly. Already he was seeing the light!

He stared at me for a minute, then nodded thoughtfully.

Chapter 8

The following Thursday before school, I staggered into the nurse's office, one hand on my stomach.

Bethanny was spraying Lysol on a counter and mopping it up with a paper towel. "Lori!" she cried, flying over and taking my arm. "What happened? Were you hit by a car?"

"No," I groaned. "It's just a bad stomach-ache. Could I lie down for a few minutes?"

"Of course," she said, helping me over to the first of three beds. "Oh, Lori, you poor, poor thing! How can I help?" She perched on the side of the bed.

This would not do at all.

"There's nothing you can do, Bethanny. It will ease up if I just lie quietly for a few minutes and don't talk."

Bethanny jumped up from the bed as if it

were on fire. "Oh, of course! How could I have been so thoughtless? Let me just get a summary slip and I'll leave you alone." She reached up and grabbed a pre-printed pad of forms and the plastic box from a shelf near the bed. She tore a form from the pad.

Then, very conveniently, she left the pad and the box on the little table next to the bed I was lying on.

And *then*, to my utter delight, she drew the full length curtain that separated the bed area from the rest of the office. It was as if she were a co-conspirator in this thing!

I heard her sit down at the nurse's deck and start typing. Then she stopped. "Just one more thing, Lori, and I won't bother you again," she called softly. "How do you spell your last name?"

"L-A-I-G-E-N," I called feebly, pawing feverishly through the summary slips in the box. "*Lucky* Laigen," I muttered.

A half hour later, Kerry was waiting for me outside my homeroom. "Well, did you get a good look at one of the slips?"

"Better than that." I waved a blank one under her nose. "There was a whole padful of them. All I have to do is photocopy this one as many times as we need it. And look at this — "

I opened my hand to show her the seven names I'd written on my palm. "These are the people, not including me, whom Bethanny had written summary slips on this week. Hers are really easy to pick out, since she's the only one who types hers." Kerry and I rolled our eyes at each other.

"Did you get a good look at the typewriter?" Kerry asked.

"That's the best news of all. The nurse's office has a Smith-Corona 2500, just like the one my mom used to use before she bought the computer. I'm almost positive it's still out in our garage."

That day at lunch, I left Big Guy in the student quad for a few minutes and went into the cafeteria, ostensibly to buy soup, which you couldn't get in the "cold lunch line," outside.

It took a while, but I finally spotted Bethanny at a table in the furthest corner of the room. She was sitting with two other quiet, mousy types I'd never noticed around school before. The three of them didn't seem to be talking, just smiling and nodding at each other as they took little bites of their sandwiches or dainty sips of milk.

My tiny little camera of a brain photographed their location.

The next day, Friday, at lunch, Kerry sauntered up to Big Guy and me at our usual bench. She usually ate lunch with Dieter and his swim team crowd.

"Lori, Ms. Toffler wants to meet with us in front of the teachers' lounge for just a couple of minutes," Kerry said. "I think she's going to put us in charge of that field trip to the Old Globe Theater to see *King Lear*."

I faked a groan and a sigh. "Be right back," I said to Big Guy. He didn't know about any of our sabotage plans for getting Bethanny out of the nurse's office. No matter how many times I reminded Kerry and myself that we were only out to save Bethanny's life, she and I were still on massive guilt trips because of the underhanded methods we had to use. And I figured — why give Big Guy a case of the guilts, too?

"Did you bring it?" I asked Kerry as soon as we were out of Big Guy's earshot.

She nodded, drew a clipboard from her book bag, and handed it to me. There was a piece of graph paper on it, with some important-looking squiggles and arrows and a bunch of numbers.

"Did you bring the new summary slips?" Kerry asked.

I waved the neatly typed packet of them at her.

Once inside the cafeteria, we headed directly

for Bethanny at her corner table. Her two mouse pals were with her.

She seemed flattered to see us as she introduced them. "We'd love to have you join us for lunch! Oh, but don't feel you have to — "

"Can't today, Bethanny," I interrupted, sitting down across the table from her. Kerry remained standing. "But we could really use your help on something for a minute."

"I'd be glad to help! Oh, whatever it is, just say, and I'll be happy to do — "

"Actually we need the help of all *three* of you," Kerry said. "We're doing a science project on extra-sensory perception."

"Yeah. ESP. And we'd like you guys to be test subjects," I said.

All three of them nodded enthusiastically, eyes wide with interest.

I gave each girl a blank sheet of notebook paper. "Okay, here's what I need you to do. First, close your eyes tight."

They did so.

"Now, I want you to sit there and think very hard about the two other girls you're sitting with."

I was touched to see Bethanny's forehead wrinkle up furiously as she gave my command her complete concentration.

Kerry took that opportunity to go through

Bethanny's stack of books. She removed an envelope that was marked "MR. FREDERICKS" in thick red felt pen.

"Now, I'm going to give you a word, and I want you to write down the first word that enters your mind after you hear that word," I said. "We're going to see how many of your words are the same. But keep your eyes closed, okay? Kerry will make sure you're writing on the paper and not on the table." Even though Kerry was busily rifling through the envelope and replacing some of the old summary slips with new ones.

"Ready for the first word?" I asked.

The girls nodded, eyes scrunched shut.

"Cat."

I had to give them six more words before Kerry could complete her mission and replace the envelope among Bethanny's books.

"Okay, you can open your eyes."

The girls were thrilled that all three of them had written down two of the same words — "dog" when I said "cat" and "white" when I said "black."

"That's the best anyone's done all day. It seems you girls have a measurable amount of ESP," I said solemnly, putting several totally meaningless scribbles on the clipboard.

When we left them, the three girls were chattering happily.

"That was like taking candy from a Bethanny," Kerry said. "It's gonna work this time. I can just feel it."

I laughed. "I was just thinking the same thing. We must have ESP."

On Fridays after school, Big Guy and I always went to the Corvette Café with a bunch of people, so I didn't get home that day until close to five.

When I came into the house, I found Bethanny huddled on our family room couch, crying into her hands. My mother was patting her shoulder, clucking gentle words, and trying to feed her hot tea with honey.

"Oh, no! What's the matter?" I asked, though I had some inkling, believe me.

"No one's home next door, and I found Bethanny sitting all alone on her front porch, crying as if her heart would break," my mother said. "Seems she had a pretty bad blow this afternoon."

I knelt down in front of her. "What happened, Bethanny? You were fine at lunch."

"I g-g-got fired from the n-n-nurse's office!" she sobbed.

I bit my lip to hold back a yelp of relief. "But why?" I finally managed to say.

My mother handed me several of the summary slips. "It seems somebody substituted bogus summary slips for the ones Bethanny originally typed up. And they got all the way to the principal."

I picked up the first one off the stack and forced myself to read it, thankful that Kerry and I had already howled over it and I could therefore keep a straight face.

STUDENT NAME: *Merry Stephens*
SYMPTOMS: *Talks too much; talks about only one thing — herself; won't let anyone else get in a word edgewise.*
DIAGNOSIS: *Boringitis*
ADVICE OR TREATMENT: *Told to shut up!*
PRECAUTIONS: *Do not get stuck talking to this person at a party!*

I managed to make a few indignant noises as I flipped through the rest of the bogus slips, which contained similar witticisms. I faked a gasp when I came to the one about me. The diagnosis had been "Swelled head." The symptoms? "Holds nose in air; addicted to mirrors; blurred vision when it come to seeing herself."

104

Advice or treatment? "Deflate ego." I'd included that one just to throw suspicion off myself, should Bethanny finally have begun to wise up.

But not to worry. When she saw me reading that one, she burst into new tears. "Oh, Lori, I didn't want you to see that one! Oh, how terrible."

"Is that what you think of me? That I'm conceited?" I asked in a small, hurt voice.

My mother threw me an odd look. I'd never been the type to use a small, hurt voice — not even as a toddler. "Bethanny didn't write those, Lori!" my mother said. She had to nearly shout to be heard over Bethanny's wails of despair.

"The p-p-principal yelled at Mrs. McSween, and she y-y-yelled at me!" Bethanny sobbed. "She said that if this was my idea of a joke . . . it was s-s-sick!"

"Sounds like something a nurse would say," I said.

Again, my mother shot me a gauging, penetrating look. She was getting suspicious. "Well, Bethanny honey, it looks like you were the victim of somebody who was out to get your job," she said.

I opened my mouth to agree, then thought better of it. Agreeing too easily with my mom's theory might really start her wondering if I was involved. And I did not want my mother in on this. She would be appalled by my methods, regardless of my good intentions. "There isn't exactly a waiting list of people panting to work in the nurse's office, Mom," I said. That did the trick. The suspicion in her eyes died.

"Look, Bethanny," I said, "if you're worried about this going on your school transcript or something, forget it. My brother, Kevin, went and checked to see if his being vice-president is on his student record and it's not. The school doesn't put extracurricular stuff on there."

"Which really upset Kevin," my mom added. "He wants to get into Stanford, and he thought having it on his official record that he was a v.p. would give him extra points with the admissions committee."

Bethanny wiped her eyes with a pink handkerchief and shook her head. "I don't care about my student record. What matters is that I let the nurse down. At least she *thinks* I did. And that those poor, sick people — including you, Lori — were ridiculed."

But of course. What reaction had I expected from her?

I sighed. "Well, nobody has seen these except us three, McSween, and the principal. Don't worry about the ridicule part."

I got up and left the room, forcing a few sighs and sympathetic clicks of my tongue until I was out of earshot.

Then I raced up the stairs, slammed my bedroom door, leaped onto the bed, and smothered a whoop in my pillow. This time I was unmoved by Bethanny's tears, so relieved was I that she was going to live, live, live! After all, now that her days were no longer numbered, she'd have a zillion other opportunities to prove herself at school.

I grabbed the phone and called Kerry. "We did it! We saved her life!" I shouted to her in a whisper. "Get ready for tonight, pal, 'cause we're gonna party!"

Specifically, we partied at Leslie Gambini's house. She had a party at least once a month.

"You're certainly in a good mood," Big Guy said to me after I'd not only danced to the old Rolling Stones' tune "Start Me Up" but also sung it at the top of my lungs. "What are you celebrating?"

People kept asking me that question all night, and I answered with real vague and corny stuff like, "I'm celebrating life." Every time Kerry would walk past us with Dieter, we'd flash each other the A-OK sign.

Early on, Darryl Combs brought up what he

called Joanne Marsh's "latest hate letter to males," meaning her latest essay in the school paper. This was her second to be published, the first having revolved around the fact that not one guy in the history of our school had ever volunteered to work in the nurse's office. *Why are males so afraid to let down their macho, chest-thumping guards?* she'd asked in that one. *Showing that you're capable of a little compassion, a little caring is not wimpy.*

"Joanne Marsh really must have gotten burned by some guy to keep coming up with the junk she's writing," Darryl said. "She hates men."

"No, she doesn't," Selena Mendez said. "I saw her at the Ken Cinema a couple of weeks ago with Brian Cosgrove and they were holding hands and sit — "

"Save-the-Whales Cosgrove?" jeered Jon Dalrymple, Selena's boyfriend. "Perfect match. They can bore and annoy each other to death about their causes and spare the rest of us."

"Anyway, she didn't come up with the stuff in her latest essay on her own," Selena said. "She got it right out of *Psychology Today*, and she gave the magazine credit. I admit I thought her first essay was sort of heavy-handed, but this latest piece — "

"Was based on the research of two female professors," cut in Jon, "who are no doubt also man-haters taking their anger out on all men just because they got stood up on a date or something."

"You're crazy," Selena said. "Their work was based on *hundreds* of conversations they observed. And all they said was that men interrupt women in four out of five conversations, while women almost never interrupt men, even when — "

"Those professors probably made the women in the studies say such outrageous things that the men *had* to interrupt them," Jon said.

"Do you realize you've just interrupted me three times in a row?" Selena said sweetly to much laughter.

I heard other references to Joanne's article throughout the night, mostly girls teasing guys to "Quit interrupting!" But I was so happy that night, so full of a-job-well-done satisfaction that I didn't even notice that it was the first party I'd been to in four months in which there wasn't a single mention of my own regular newspaper contribution, "Lori's Listening."

Kerry spent the night at my house. We were still so keyed up and proud of ourselves that we stayed up all night, gorging on frozen French-bread pizzas, brownies my mother had made three days before, and plenty of caffeine-laden Coke, which kept us going. We talked about almost everybody we'd ever met since third grade, did some wonderful imitations, and laughed our heads off.

"This is the slumber party we didn't have at the Marshes' house," Kerry said, holding up her Coke bottle for a toast.

When the sun started to come up, both of us were finally lying down on our beds, and the silences between comments were growing longer and longer. My eyes felt gritty, heavy. I closed them.

Suddenly, Kerry sat bolt upright. "What was that?" she whispered.

"What was what?"

"There's somebody outside."

I yawned. "It's probably just the paper boy."

"Lori, check, okay? I heard whispering. Maybe they're trying to figure out the easiest way to break into the house!"

I sighed and crept over to the window. "It's just Bethanny, saying good-bye to her cats. Wonder where she's going so early on a Saturday morning when there's — "

My heart stopped.

Bethanny was wearing a candy striper's uniform.

Chapter 9

Well, that was it for me. I had to give up. There was no way I could sabotage Bethanny's stint as a candy striper at St. Ann's Hospital without risking arrest. And besides, there are at least 50 other hospitals and convalescent hospitals in San Diego County. Even if I could have succeeded in getting her fired from St. Ann's, she'd probably just continue doggedly on from hospital to hospital, and I would end up dying of frustration, creative burnout, and exhaustion before I could save her from dying herself.

I may have given up trying to keep her away from sick people, but I didn't stop worrying. I worried about her constantly. I always watched for her to come out of her house in the mornings, and if she was leaving without a sweater I'd bark down at her to go put one on.

I bought and presented her with big bottles of megadose C and other vitamins, explaining that my dad got them free at work.

Whenever I'd pass her in the halls at school, I'd silently make a handwashing gesture, and she'd scurry towards a restroom or whip out a prepackaged "moistened towelette" — a box of which had also been a "gift" from me. I occasionally stuffed appropriate newspaper clippings into her locker — i.e. "NURSES FOUND TO HAVE MUCH HIGHER INCIDENCE OF RESPIRATORY ILLNESS."

Anybody else would have swatted me away, dismissed me as a nutcase, a squawking, paranoid, compulsive, annoying germ freak. Not Bethanny, of course. Although she seemed rather perplexed by my actions, she accepted all of this with her usual sweetness and gratitude.

And then came the mid-March day on which something so monumental happened that it drove all thoughts of Bethanny from my mind completely: Big Guy asked me to come to Sunday dinner at his house.

I remember with utter clarity the day he asked me. It started, quite as usual, with my calling down a sweater/vitamin reminder to Bethanny, after which Kerry and I snuck peaks out my window at the latest of "Megan's Morons." That day's moron was an achingly gorgeous Jon Bon Jovi look-alike except that he had short hair.

Kerry sighed. "How can he — how can *any* of them — seriously consider a girl who only knows the three M words — mousse, MTV, and money?"

"Easy," I said. "She's got the three B's — blonde hair, blue eyes, and — "

"I gotcha," Kerry said, and then we both practically fell on the floor, laughing at how clever and witty we were. How could I have known that that laughter would echo tauntingly through my mind for weeks to come?

It was at lunch that Big Guy popped the question. "My mom says she knows it's awfully short notice, but she wonders if you'd like to come to dinner at our house on Sunday afternoon."

I caught my breath. He must really be serious about me to put his mother up to this! So far she had been only a voice on the phone to me. Oh, and one brief glimpse of a tall, chic woman in rose-colored Ultrasuede when I slunk past her antique shop one day, hoping to see Big Guy in there. That was before we'd starting going out together. As for Big Guy's father, an airline executive who traveled constantly, I'd never even spoken to him on the phone.

"What will I wear?" I squeaked, by way of saying yes.

Big Guy looked at me as if I were an idiot. "It doesn't matter. Anything."

Kerry, of course, understood that it *did* matter. She understood the terrifying prospect of making a good first impression on one's boyfriend's parents. On Saturday afternoon, she came over to help me choose an outfit. She was armed with her sister Jill's book about choosing clothes colors according to what "season" you are (I'm a winter). We had decided that Mrs. Grimes was the flawlessly, effortlessly fashionable type who knew a person's color season and entire recommended palette of colors at a glance. Kerry also brought along an article she'd clipped from one of the teen mags about what wearing certain colors supposedly said about you.

"How about my black suede vest and pants?" I said, whipping it out of the closet and holding it in front of me.

"Uh-uh," Kerry said. "The books says black is a good color for a winter, but the article says that people who wear black are fascinated with death." She snickered. "Imagine, Mrs. Grimes would know that about you without your even mentioning your collection of tombstones."

Sighing, I rehung the black suede outfit in the closet and took out a deep purple oversized silk shirt.

"Nope," Kerry said, shaking the article at me. "According to this, people who wear purple like to make other people miserable."

The trouble with that article was that it had something negative to say about every single color of the rainbow. It even got its digs in about various prints, such as plaids and stripes. Polka dots, for example, supposedly signified phoniness in the wearer.

I finally settled on a conservative, sky-colored sweater-dress, since the article seemed to have the fewest complaints about blue (wearers were simply branded "inconsiderate").

Next, Kerry and I decided that etiquette required my bringing flowers to Mrs. Grimes. We had to go through the whole process of elimination again, thanks to a book we found in my mom's office bookcase called *The Language of Flowers*. This book said giving yellow carnations, for instance, indicated you felt "disdain" for the giftee; marigolds represented "grief"; and yellow roses "jealousy."

"Look, this is ridiculous," I said at one point, slamming the book shut in frustration. "A pretty flower is a pretty flower. Mrs. Grimes is too sophisticated to be superstitious about flowers, let alone to own or even read this dumb book. Same goes for that stupid article about what colors mean. Let's just go to Mission Hills Flowers and buy whatever looks good, smells nice, and costs cheap."

Kerry shook her head. "Aren't you the person who's been yelling at me for two months about not taking any chances?"

So we ended up convincing Kevin (via ten bucks plus gas money) to drive us all the way up to the Poway Nurseryland because that store seemed to be the only one in San Diego County that had any white chrysanthemums, which supposedly represented "truth."

The next afternoon, I nearly dropped the pot of them on the Grimes' front porch, so nervous was I when Big Guy's dad threw open the front door.

"Oh, white chrysanthemums!" Mrs. Grimes cried, coming into the entryway to meet me. "The flower of truth." I was too busy trying to keep my smile from shaking to say a silent prayer of thanks to Kerry.

Big Guy came in, and Mrs. Grimes led us to the family room, where an NBA game was on TV. She snapped the set off and left us so she could finish cooking dinner.

Silver-haired Mr. Grimes was one of those tall, ramrod-straight, thin-lipped executive types you expect to be stern and humorless. But he turned out to be a very hearty, macho, and warm guy. He switched the TV back on the instant Mrs. Grimes was out of earshot but he tried very hard not to let his eyes stray to it very often as we chatted about my parents, school, and the school football team's past season.

When Mrs. Grimes called us to the table, she ordered Mr. Grimes to turn the TV off. He supposedly stayed behind to do so. But as we all sat down at the table I could still hear a low murmur of the basketball game coming from the family room, although Mrs. Grimes apparently couldn't. Suddenly, I began to feel more at home, more relaxed. Secretly turning the TV set down instead of off during dinner was an old trick of my own dad.

Dinner was a tasty pork roast served with a rich, chunky, cinnamonny applesauce, cheesy scalloped potatoes, and a tossed green salad with generous slices of ripe avocado. Mr. and Mrs. Grimes drank wine, and Big Guy and I were served sparkling cider in the same kind of crystal wineglasses his parents were using. I thought that was a classy touch.

"So," Mrs. Grimes said to me, "I understand

you two met when Brook was assigned to be your math tutor."

I stared at her blankly. Brook?

Big Guy groaned. "It's *B.G.*, Mom. How many times do I have to remind you?"

Mrs. Grimes blushed and dabbed at her lips with a mint-green linen napkin. "Oh, I'm sorry, honey," she said to him. "Sometimes it just slips out, even after all these years."

I turned to Big Guy. "The B in B.G. stands for Brook?" Why had I never thought to ask him what those initials meant? I guess I'd always assumed he had some run-of-the-mill name. Like Brian. Or Bob.

"Brook Gregory," Mrs. Grimes answered for him. "Brook Gregory Grimes." She sighed and smiled. "It has such a nice ring to it."

Big Guy scowled at her. "As you know, I prefer B.G., thank you very much."

"The minute Brooke Shields came on the scene, B.G. insisted we stop calling him Brook," Mrs. Grimes said to me, sighing again. "Before that, Brook was always considered a male name."

"I think you're thinking of the name Brock, Mom," Big Guy grumbled. "You confused Brook with Brock."

Mr. Grimes cleared his throat. "No, B.G., you're confusing Brock with Rock," he said.

They kept arguing good-naturedly. Somebody said something about "Broderick" and "Roderick." But I just sat there stunned, barely hearing them.

Because it had hit me like a ton of bricks: There's a Brook in *Little Women*. Mr. Brook. He is the tutor — the *tutor* — of a character named Laurie, who lives next door to the March girls. Oh, sure, the Lori/Laurie next-door neighbor parallel had occurred to me before, but I had dismissed it as having no relevance, mainly because the Laurie in the book is male (Laurie is short for Laurence). But the sudden discovery that there was also a tutor named Brook in *this* story — *my* life — was too eerie, too uncanny to be considered just another coincidence. Especially when I added it to the mountain of other details the March family and the Marsh family had in common.

But it wasn't the fact that both the live Lori and the fictional Laurie had tutors named Brook that was making me grip the edge of the Grimes' table, certain that if I let go I'd keel over in a dead faint. It was the memory that *the Brook in the book goes on to meet, fall in love with, and marry Meg!*

Chapter 10

"Is something wrong, Lori?"

I had to shake myself hard, like a wet dog. Looking up, I found Mrs. Grimes staring at me with wide-eyed worry. Lifting a forkful of pork to her nose, she sniffed it suspiciously.

"No, no, I'm fine," I croaked at her. "Everything's fine." I reached for my glass, hoping that a sip of cider would ease my throat, which was swollen shut with anxiety. I ended up downing it, unable to control the noise I made as I swallowed — "gunk, gunk, gunk."

Mrs. Grimes' mouth was only a quarter-inch away from depicting the expression "hanging open in surprise."

I turned toward the males. They weren't paying any attention to us. Instead, they were in the middle of a heated discussion about an upcoming Hagler-Hearns boxing match.

I stared at Big Guy, unaware that I was pointing a fork at him as if it were loaded. Surely as he read *Little Women* it must have struck him as a spooky coincidence that the book contained a Brook and a Laurie, too. So why hadn't he mentioned it to me? Why had he never added that parallel to all the parallels I'd already collected and presented to him? And then a simple answer occurred to me.

"Hagler might be a better boxer," Big Guy was saying to his dad, "but he'll never be able to take the kind of punishment Hearns dishes out. Especially if — "

"I have to know, Big Guy," I interrupted in a strangled voice. "How far have you read in *Little Women*?"

Mr. Grimes stared at his son with an expression that was a mixture of astonishment and concern.

Big Guy was unable to look at his father. "I'm only up to the part where the guy next door — Laurie — is meeting the March girls," he said, pushing a piece of meat around on his plate.

Mr. Grimes seemed to recover his poise, evidently having concluded that *Little Women* was a school assignment. "And you thought Brook was an effeminate name for a guy, B.G. The name 'Laurie' makes Brook sound like Arnold Schwarzenegger." He threw his head back and let loose a string of hearty, macho haw-haw-haws.

"Laurie is short for Laurence," Big Guy muttered.

But all I could think of was: *He hasn't gotten to the Brook part in the book yet.*

I don't remember much else about the meal, except that each of the others said "Earth to Lori" at least once apiece. Oh, yeah, I do also remember picking up with my hands what I thought — in my zombified state — was a brownie. It was only after I'd taken a big bite of it that I discovered it was actually a rather runny piece of chocolate mousse. Hastily, I dropped it back on the dessert plate, wiped my dripping fingers on my napkin, and looked around to see if any of the others had noticed this gaffe. Big Guy and his dad were oblivious, discussing some NFL coach. But it was obvious Mrs. Grimes was making a supreme effort not to stare at me as she fed herself dainty bites of chocolate mousse with a tiny silver dessert fork.

All in all, you could say I blew that all-important first meeting of my boyfriend's parents rather spectacularly.

But I couldn't help it. Because this new development made it ominously clear that I was in danger of losing that boyfriend no matter what his parents' opinion of me . . . losing that boyfriend to Megan Marsh! I could think of nothing else.

I was dying to get out of there and call Kerry to discuss the situation, and only with super-human willpower did I keep myself from drumming my fingers on the table when Mrs. Grimes poured second cups of coffee for Mr. Grimes and herself. I stifled a scream of frustration when she poured thirds.

Finally, she got up and went to the kitchen with a few plates. I leaped up from my chair and raced after her, arms piled with dirty dishes.

"Oh, please don't bother," she said. "Clearing the table is B.G.'s job."

"In that case," I said, "I really have to be going. My mother has a tight deadline to meet tomorrow and I promised I'd help her with the project this evening."

Knowing I'd be out of there within three minutes, I did my best to be gracious and warm to Mr. and Mrs. Grimes. I gushed about the food, the furniture, the location of the house, the weather, and just about everything else as I edged purposefully toward the front door.

Once outside, I tried to talk Big Guy out of driving me home, making an inane remark about the fresh air being good for creativity. What I was secretly hoping to do was race straight over to Kerry's. But Big Guy insisted, and I didn't want to have a fight in front of his parents.

He drove very slowly, his jaw set with excessive rigidity, his lips tight. I knew he was waiting for me to ask him what the matter was, but I wasn't about to do that until I'd come up with a logical reason to explain my strange behavior at the dinner table. A little voice in my head was screaming at me to not tell him the truth. The little voice also promised that it would explain the reason for this later.

Big Guy gave up waiting for me to make the first move. "You hate my parents," he burst out.

I eased across the bench seat and snuggled up next to him. "No, I don't. Your dad is nice and funny. And your mom's real smart and sweet. Plus she's a terrific cook, and her decorating is — "

"You can quit gushing now, Lori, since we're alone," he snapped. "Just tell me why, if you liked them so much, you just sat there like a zombie through the entire dinner."

"Because I don't know anything about boxing," I snapped back.

"Listen, I only brought up the Hearns-

Hagler match to fill in the long, deadly silences. Meanwhile, you were off in some Never-Never Land, swaying in your seat and practically drooling."

His words gave me sudden inspiration. "It's just that I felt so sick," I said.

His eyebrows shot up.

"No, wait, I don't mean the food made me sick," I said. "Actually, I felt pretty queasy before I even got to your house. Must be that bug that's going around school."

He stiffened, a sort of automatic keep-your-germs-away reflex, but he also blew out a sigh of relief. "Oh, so that was the problem," he said as I moved back over to the passenger side. "I think my mom will understand that. She felt pretty crummy herself a couple of days ago. You should have said something."

Instead of replying, I clutched at my stomach and groaned. Big Guy clicked his tongue sympathetically.

The truth was, I really *did* feel sick: sick with worry that I was going to lose him and sick to death of the Marshes and the way they were mangling my life.

Twenty minutes later, Kerry flopped back on her bed in exasperation. "This time, I think you've gone too far with the book thing," she said. "Now just relax and forget it, kid. I mean, Megan and Big Guy are only sixteen! Do you honestly believe either set of parents would allow them to get married at that age?"

"Reread the book!" I wailed. "In the book, they wait for three or four years so that Brook can sock away bucks to buy them a house while Meg socks away doilies in her hope chest!"

That little tidbit seemed to take Kerry aback. She was silent for a long minute, pulling absently at her chenille bedspread. "Look, it just can't happen," she finally said slowly. "He would never go for someone like Megan."

"Oh, yes he would! Didn't I ever tell you he went out with Reesa Tokay when they were sophomores? Only one time, but still: Reesa's even stupider than Megan. And she's not half as gorgeous." I sat down at Kerry's desk and dropped my face into my hands. "Oh, Kerry, I don't have a chance. Amanda told me that Megan's gotten every guy she's ever gone after. That is, the rare times she's had to go after a guy, since they're usually falling all over her."

Kerry came over and took me by the shoulders. "Now stop it! Stop it! Everything in that book that's come true for the Marches hasn't come true for the Marshes and you know it. Look at Bethanny, for example. She never did get sick, did she? And after all that worrying and rushing around you did."

"She didn't get sick *yet*," I wailed. "You just wait."

"Anyway, Big Guy and Megan haven't even met each other, have they?" Kerry said. "How can you fall madly in love with someone you don't even know exists?"

Suddenly, the little voice inside my head said: "She's right. That's the key."

I stared at her for a long minute. Then I got up from the chair and started pacing. "Well, that's it, then. That's the answer. I have to keep them from meeting each other. I have to rewrite the plot."

Kerry flopped facedown on her bed with a groan.

"And while I'm doing that," I continued, ignoring her lack of enthusiasm, "I'm also gonna have to keep him from finishing *Little Women*."

"Why?" she muttered, mouth pressed against the bedspread.

"Because sooner or later he would stumble upon the Brook-plus-Meg subplot. And he'd be dying to meet the *real* Meg just out of curiosity. He's only human. Oh, me and my big mouth! If only I had never told him about all this!"

"If only you had never told *me*," came Kerry's muffled cry of anguish.

* * *

"Listen, I was walking past the school newspaper office last Friday afternoon, and I heard a terrible fight going on in there."

I stifled a groan and turned around. Nicole Craig had sidled up beside me in the deserted school corridor. I couldn't even leave class with a bathroom pass, I thought grumpily, without somebody bugging me to report gossip. Hastily, I stepped away from Big Guy's locker and tried not to look guilty.

"You don't seem very interested," Nicole said, her voice flat with disappointment. "Oh, wait . . . maybe that's it. Maybe you just don't print gossip about the newspaper staff. Well, that's not fair!" She narrowed her green eyes at me.

I sighed. "I do *too* print stuff about the newspaper staff. So go ahead, hit me. Whatcha got?"

Nicole moved closer. "Well, it was a shouting match between Katie Tarantino — she's still the editor, right? — and that new girl who's been writing the essays. Joanne Marsh?"

At last my curiosity was awakened. "Really? Go on."

"Well, I didn't hear the whole thing, but Katie shouted, 'When I want your opinion, Joanne, I'll ask for it!' Then Joanne yelled something like, 'That doesn't change the fact

128

that it's silly and a waste of space!' And then Mrs. Caprice shouted at Katie to shut up."

"You mean Joanne," I said. "Mrs. Caprice shouted at *Joanne* to shut up, right?"

"Nope. It was 'Shut up, Katie!' "

My eyebrows shot up in surprise. "Did you hear anything else?"

"Then both Katie and Joanne started talking at the same time, and one of them shouted 'I refuse to do it!' but I couldn't tell which one," Nicole said. "Then Katie just stormed out of the room. And that was it."

I nodded thoughtfully. "I bet I can guess what that was all about. I've heard Mrs. Caprice really likes Joanne's writing and has been urging Katie to give her more assignments. Katie probably assigned Joanne a topic that wasn't 'relevant,' to use Joanne's own favorite word. And Joanne refused to do it. Interesting."

Nicole's eyes were wide and bright. "So are you going to use my tip?"

I stood there and wondered with which girl Nicole had a bone to pick — Katie or Joanne? Whichever it was, Nicole no doubt figured the report of a shrewish cat fight would lessen the girl in the eyes of some boy of mutual interest. Was I jaded or what?

"Uh-uh," I said. "I can't run it."

"But why? You said stuff about newspaper people was fair game."

"Yeah, except for stuff about the editor or the faculty adviser, both of whom figure prominently in your tip and both of whom have the power to fire me."

She twirled on her heel and stalked off down the hall. "Thanks for nothing!" she called over her shoulder.

"Same to you!"

As soon as she was around a corner, I went straight back to Big Guy's locker, worked the combination, and opened it easily. After all, I'd stood beside him a million times when he'd done it himself.

There it was — the phony *Escape from Omega II*. E.T.'s evil twin brother leered at me until the book disappeared into my book bag.

Big Guy approached me after school that day with humble eyes. "Lori . . . I . . . uh, I don't know how to tell you this . . . but I lost *Little Women*!"

Instinctively, I pulled my book bag closer to my body. Then I feigned a bit of upset: "You did? Oh, that's terrible."

He hung his head as we made our way down the crowded corridor. "I thought I put it into my locker after third period but I must have accidentally left it in study hall. I went back there just now to check but it wasn't there."

"Did you get to read much of it in study hall?" I asked.

He stopped and peered at me, puzzled. I guess it *did* seem like an irrelevant question, under the circumstances. "I didn't get to read it at all," he muttered. "Too much English homework."

I sighed with relief, but he mistook it for sadness.

"Look, I'm really, really sorry, Lori," he said. "Your mom told me a relative gave it to you when you were born, so I know how much it must have meant to you, and I intend to — "

"No!" I interrupted, as dread suddenly surged through my soul. I smelled a plan backfiring. "Actually, I couldn't stand that book because my aunt Liz gave it to me, and my aunt Liz went on to divorce my uncle Hal. My whole family despises her. So good riddance to the book. I mean, thanks for losing it!"

But it was too late.

"Don't try to make me feel better," Big Guy said. "I intend to buy you another copy. And as soon as I do, I'll finish reading it right away, even if it takes all night. It's the least I can do."

Chapter 11

In the next several days, Kerry and I bought up every single new copy of *Little Women* that was within bus range of Mission Hills. Luckily, most bookstores carried only one . . . and most of them also gave cash refunds. Every night, I'd call Big Guy and casually ask, "Where did you look for the book today?" He'd mention the stores he'd called or visited — without success, of course — and the next day Kerry and/or I would return the books to those establishments. That's why, in the end, my college fund was permanently down only by the amount I spent on bus fares.

Big Guy exploded in frustration on Wednesday evening. "Village Books said they sold the only copy they had just this afternoon. And, like all the other places, they said they could order it for me, but that it would take six weeks! How long can it take to mail a book? Where is the publishing company — Antarctica? Well, they can just forget it!"

On Saturday, I pulled a crafty little maneuver. Big Guy asked me to accompany him to three major malls in search of the book. After we entered each mall bookstore, I said "Why don't you go to the counter and ask if they have it? Meanwhile, I'll go back and start looking for it." Then I simply hid the book behind a row of others before Big Guy and the clerk appeared. Cost to me: nothing.

On Saturday night, after going to the Reuben H. Fleet Space Theater, we sat in his car about a block south of my house, our arms around each other.

"I'm sorry, babe, that I haven't been able to get my hands on another copy of *Little Women*," he said.

"Forget it," I said. "Anyway, that whole thing about the Marches and the Marshes being parallel families or something was ridiculous." My voice sounded high and phony, but he didn't seem to notice.

He kissed me. "Doesn't matter," he murmured. "I mean . . . I'm glad you've come to your senses and that you're over that weird obsession. But the least I can do is to finish reading the thing, especially after I lost your copy. I'm going to check *Little Women* out of the library at school, okay? And I don't care who sees me."

I bit my lip to prevent a scream of frustration from bursting forth. "Please don't, Big Guy. It's really not neces — "

"I insist," he kept saying, no matter what I said. "It's about time I started reading the classics anyway. It'll give you and me another thing in common." Another long kiss.

He started talking about something that had happened the day before in his English class. I tuned him out and made plans to be the first person to go through the doors of the school library at seven-thirty on Monday morning.

Incidentally, we were sitting about a block south of my house because that's where I was having him drop me off these days. Same with picking me up. Obviously, I didn't want him coming anywhere near my house, where he might perchance lay eyes on marvelous Megan Marsh.

Convincing him that we could no longer have tutoring sessions at my house on Tuesday and Thursday afternoons had been easy enough. I simply told him that my mother was going to be working with one of her clients in the family room every afternoon for the next several weeks so our presence was not welcome. Big

Guy arranged for us to use a little cubicle off the school library on some days; on others he just tutored me in his car as we sat overlooking the city in a parking lot at Presidio Park.

Convincing him that he could no longer pick me up or drop me off at home, however, was a different story: I had to tell him a lie that made both of us very uncomfortable. I told him that my parents were restricting me from dating until I brought my grade up in Spanish. And that therefore Big Guy and I would have to meet secretly.

"It isn't fair," I offered in an effort to explain why I had decided to go out with him "behind their backs." "Kevin got a C in his Spanish class, too, but they're not restricting *him*. They're being sexist and unfair, so I'm not going to play fair, either."

Big Guy didn't care how I rationalized what we were doing. He said he felt terrible "cheating on" my parents and especially my dad, whom he was crazy about. Whenever we were in public — like at the Corvette or the movies or wherever — Big Guy looked around nervously, guiltily, constantly, making sure my parents weren't in sight.

"How can two people as highly educated as your parents believe you're spending all this time at Kerry's studying?" he kept fretting.

Kerry, by the way, found the situation highly amusing. "I've heard of people who lie to their parents about where they're going, but you must be the first person in history who is telling her parents the truth but lying to her boyfriend about what she's telling them. Weird stuff."

I didn't find it amusing at all. I felt as guilty and terrible as Big Guy did, for lying to him. And I, too, was nervous that we'd run into my parents — nervous because if we did they'd act friendly and nice and normal rather than furious, as Big Guy feared.

But I felt somewhat vindicated for the crummy things I was doing when, one afternoon, I stood at my bedroom window and watched Megan Marsh charm the daylights out of Mr. Monahan, our cranky and intimidating mailman. He was the type of guy who answered your "Good morning" by snapping something like, "It'll be a good morning when the government puts an end to Saturday mail deliveries." Spitefully, he also often inserted important letters and bills inside junk-mail catalogs, making it necessary to carefully shake out all junk mail before tossing it.

When I first caught a glimpse of him and Megan standing together on the Marshes' driveway, I picked up the phone to call the paramedics. It took another cautious look for me to determine that that grimace on Old Man Monahan's face was a *smile* and not evidence that he was suffering a heart attack. He and Megan chatted for about ten minutes before he *kissed her cheek* and went on with his rounds. I figured that if Megan could conquer a creepy, old, mean guy like Monahan, she would be able to knock over someone as nice and open-minded as Big Guy with a feather.

To my dismay, when Big Guy couldn't get *Little Women* in our school library (thanks to me), he announced that he'd try to get one through the San Diego Public Library. That made it necessary for Kerry and me to start on a whole new round of bus trips — this time to every branch library within a ten-mile radius. A couple of times, we secretly made it in and out of a particular branch just ten minutes before Big Guy did.

These library trips also made it necessary to invent a whole new bunch of phony excuses for Big Guy as to where I was going after school every day. Add this to the frustration he was feeling about not being able to get the book and his guilt about the "sneaking around" he thought we were doing at night, and the result was a boy who was acting sulkier and more withdrawn as each day passed. I hung in there, telling myself that things would get better between us as soon as he gave up the search for *Little Women* and I could relax my schedule a bit.

All of my frantic running around had another effect: I barely saw any of the Marsh girls for almost two weeks. That's why it was such a staggering blow when Bethanny was hospitalized.

It happened on a damp, starless spring night. Voices in the driveway below woke me up. On my way to the window, I looked at my clock-radio: It was almost three. Aunt Marsh, Megan, and Amanda were hustling a well-bundled Bethanny into Aunt Marsh's car. Then Aunt Marsh laid scratch as she drove away.

I opened my window. "What's the matter?" I called down softly to Megan and Amanda, who were still standing in the driveway, looking after the car.

Amanda pulled her fuzzy pink robe tighter around herself. "Bethanny could hardly breathe," she said in a tight, scared little voice. "Aunt Marsh thinks she has pneumonia!"

I slammed the window shut and flew down to join them in the driveway.

"How did this happen?" I demanded, voice thick with tears. "How could this happen?"

Megan, too, was tearful. "She caught the flu somewhere, and it just got worse and worse.

Now this." Megan looked goddess-like in a velvety white robe that swirled out around her legs and nearly touched the tops of her tiny bare feet.

"Hasn't she been taking her vitamins?" I barked, pacing the driveway. "Hasn't she been washing her hands? How could this happen? How could you let this happen?"

They watched me with shocked expressions. Obviously, they hadn't expected this intense a reaction from someone who didn't seem all that close to their sister.

"I don't think Bethanny's getting pneumonia had anything to do with her habits," Amanda snapped. "What made her flu get worse was that she just refused to stay in bed."

"Yeah," Megan said. "She insisted on going to school and stuff because she's helping a teacher with some special project. You know how she is — she's just too thoughtful and considerate for her own good!"

"It's thought*less* and *in*considerate to expose other people to a flu virus," I snapped back, the doctor's daughter. Then I pivoted on my heels and stormed back into my house.

But I spent the rest of that night crying, phoning over to the Marshes for hospital updates, and waiting for it to be reasonably late enough to call Kerry.

"This is it, she's a goner, she's gonna die just like the book said," I finally sobbed to Kerry at 6:03. "Bethanny's in Mercy Hospital with pneumonia."

Kerry seemed too stunned to speak. She didn't even yell at me for calling so early. "I'm calling the hospital," she said after a long minute of silence. She hung up.

A few minutes later, the phone rang. "She's 'stable,'" Kerry reported. "Or that's the hospital lingo. I asked the nurse to translate, and she said Bethanny has improved a lot." Kerry blew out a sigh of relief.

I just started sobbing again. "That's what happened in the book, too. She recovers, but she's never the same. And soon enough, she croaks."

Exasperated with me, Kerry hung up.

Then Amanda called. "Bethanny's much better!" she sang. "But she has to stay in the hospital for a while."

My breath caught in my throat, but I stifled a sob for Amanda's sake. I felt so sorry for her. Amanda was so naive and innocent; such a good, trusting kid. She would just be smashed to bits when her beloved big sister died. Well, my role was clear. I would have to prepare her for the blow — help her buck up for the inevitability of Bethanny's death . . . without actually spelling it out for her. After all, Amanda would have plenty of time to mourn when it actually happened. Why start her suffering now?

I took a deep breath. "Can you stop by for a few minutes before you leave for school, Amanda? Say, in about an hour? I want to lend you a couple books I think you'll find helpful."

When I got off the phone, I raced around to every bookcase in the house and finally decided on *The Ann Landers Encyclopedia* and Kahlil Gibran's *The Prophet*. Both of these books had specific sections relating to death and dying. But I skipped those and instead bookmarked and highlighted with a yellow pen several vague philosophical passages about coping with any kind of loss in life. The Ann Landers material, for example, started out *No one knows why life must be so punishing to some of God's finest creatures.* . . . Even jaded old me found the passage somewhat comforting.

When Amanda came by, I pressed the books on her, urging her to read the marked parts for "your future growth and fulfillment."

Well, she certainly wasn't Bethanny. Bethanny would have taken the books and read them — puzzled but without protest or question.

"I get my future growth and fulfillment from Wonder Bread," Amanda said. "Look, Lori, this is nice of you, but what gives? I mean, how come you're suddenly so interested in my mental health? And are the books all that necessary? Believe me, I already have enough books to read, thanks to homework."

I shook my head, refused to give her a straight answer, and once again urged her to read the books. I added a vague, flowery phrase about how she would need to become "a willow tree that bends but doesn't yield to the wind," badly butchering something I remembered from the Gibran book.

Amanda stared at me, wide-eyed, then took off with a hurried good-bye.

After school that day, I was up in my bedroom with the window open when I heard Amanda's voice. She was down in the Marshes' side yard, sketching a friend.

"The girl next door is really weird and spooky," Amanda told her friend, shuddering.

I didn't care what she thought. For days after that I just moped around, feeling depressed and helpless about Bethanny. It didn't matter how upbeat the reports about her were — that she was "really perking up," "eating like a horse," and "coming home any day." I just kept picturing her eventual return home — a pale, sickly version of her former self . . . doomed to die.

One of the worst things about this period was that I couldn't tell Big Guy what had me so down. He'd finally given up his search for *Little Women*, and if I told him the truth about my depression I would risk rekindling his interest in the book. This time, I might not be able to get all the books out of the libraries and stores in time. He might get ahold of one, find out about the Brook-plus-Meg thing, and . . . well, I just couldn't bear the thought of losing not just Bethanny but, in a poetic sense, Big Guy, too. Now that Bethanny was gravely ill I was more paranoid than ever about the book's power of prediction.

"What's wrong? What's wrong?" Big Guy kept asking me, whether we were at school, the Corvette, the mall, the movies, or his car a block away from my house.

I'd murmur a barrage of complaints about my parents, my brother, my column, school, Kerry, the stupidity of some sitcoms, and even the weather, but not once did I mention any of the Marshes.

And not once did he believe me, I could tell. He'd finally give up trying to wheedle the real problem out of me. And he'd turn away, lips tight, silent, sulky.

Chapter 12

And then came the day I will forever remember as Black Thursday.

It was a rainy day, appropriately enough, and Kerry and I took shelter in the jammed library before school in order to finish our Spanish homework.

A piece of wadded-up paper landed on top of my notebook. Yawning, I opened it without looking up, certain it was just another gossip tip.

What school newspaper editor is having to abandon her job because her father is being transferred to Seattle? And why is said newspaper editor warning her staff that her successor, handpicked by Mrs. Caprice, is promising to wreak havoc on life as the staff now knows it?

I gasped and looked up. Katie Tarantino herself stood in front of me — my champion, my mentor, my boss. "No," I croaked, "you can't go!"

"Try telling my father that," she said with a sad smile.

"And this successor Mrs. Caprice has picked out," I said. "Please don't tell me it's — "

"You got it. Joanne Marsh," Katie snapped. "Caprice just loves her 'incisive writing and intriguing ideas,' quote unquote. It also didn't hurt that Joanne reminds Caprice of herself when she was sixteen." Katie shuddered.

"You and Joanne never did become best buddies, did you?" I said dryly.

Katie snorted. "Well, anyway, it was nice working with you." She walked away, then turned back. "Just don't be surprised if you find your column taking on a new slant. She'll probably cut your juicy tidbits to make room for her own. You know what I mean: 'What budding biologist with an IQ of 150 giggled like an idiot and professed total ignorance when jock Jamie Stephenson asked her the meaning of the term H_2O?' " Katie shuddered again and left the library.

I faced Kerry with a groan. "She's probably right."

Kerry nodded. "Joanne'll probably turn 'Lori's Listening' into 'Lori's Lecturing.' " Neither of us laughed.

It turned out to be much worse than we expected.

In Spanish, Señor Fernandez handed me a note from Mrs. Caprice that ordered me to report to the newspaper office right after school for a meeting with her and Joanne.

When I got there, Joanne acknowledged my presence with a nod, a flip of her luxuriant, dark hair, and a gesture toward a chair. She was busy arguing with Brian Cranston, the sports editor, while Mrs. Caprice looked on with an innocent smile.

"You *will* do it, Cranston, and immediately," Joanne said.

"You can't make me!" Brian shouted. "You're not being fair!"

She threw him an icy smile. "*Au contraire*, I am being extremely fair. In fact, I am probably the only editor in the history of this school to be so fair. You've heard of Title 9, haven't you?"

Brian just glared at her.

"That's the federal law making it illegal for a school to spend more money on boys' sports than on girls'," Joanne said. "Well, I'm hereby making it illegal to give more coverage to boys' sports in the school paper."

My heart began sinking at that point. Katie had been right. "Lori's Lecturing" loomed.

146

Brian's entire face was twisted in a sneer. "Do you really think people are going to care one iota that the girls' j.v. field hockey team went into overtime when they — "

"Yes!" Joanne leaned across the table until her face was close to his. "In the past, most people at this school probably didn't even know we had a j.v. field hockey team, thanks to sports editors like you." She flew over to Mrs. Caprice's desk and picked up the last issue of the paper. Holding up the back page, she thrust it in front of Brian's eyes. "Look at this! You used three full columns for a picture of a bunch of sweaty basketball jocks doing nothing but sitting on the bench." She jabbed at the extreme bottom right-hand corner of the page. "And you covered *all* of the girls' sports — volleyball, basketball, field hockey, tennis, and gymnastics — in *one paragraph, total*. Disgusting! And totally unfair!"

Joanne stomped back to Mrs. Caprice's desk and sailed the newspaper back onto it. Then she whirled around to face Brian again. "You will give equal coverage to girls' sports or you are fired."

Brian's mouth fell open, and he turned to the teacher. "Mrs. Caprice — "

She muttered something about "equality under the law."

He shook his head at the teacher in disbelief and stood up to face Joanne. "This isn't some federal law. It's just Joanne the shrew's law! And you can't fire me — I quit!"

Joanne waved a hand at him in a dismissing gesture. "Then clean out your desk," she said — rather theatrically, I might add, since none of us had a desk in the newspaper office. There were just a couple of computers and printers and the big table used by everyone.

Brian stormed from the room, and Joanne turned to me, unsmiling.

I stood up to head her off at the pass. "Look, Joanne, I can't make 'Lori's Listening' into some sort of — "

She held up her hand to stop me. "Lori, I have had quite enough fighting for one day, thank you very much. I am not going to ask you to 'make' your column into anything. I called you here to tell you that we are dropping your column from the paper, effective immediately."

Much like Brian's, my mouth dropped open. My world began to fall apart. "But — "

"I won't mince words," Joanne interrupted. "I'm sure you're adult enough to handle the truth. Which is that your column has been nothing more than a fluffy and trivial space-waster from the word go. For all of these months you have been allowed to squander valuable inches in order to either make vicious fun of or glorify a precious few — all of the above, I might add, members of the same tiny, elite group."

I tossed my head angrily. "I think the *real* problem is — "

"Please let me finish," she said. "Your column seems to pretend that the vast majority of people at this school do not even exist. In printing it, we have ignored *their* needs, Lori, while pandering to the elites. We have wasted hundreds of inches that could have been devoted to material that is more relevant or at least more helpful to *all* teens as they struggle through this miserable malady known as adolescence. Henceforth, that is exactly what we will use the space for."

Suddenly, I realized that the fight Nicole Craig had overheard between Katie and Joanne had been over me and my column. So this wasn't just some sudden or passing whim of Joanne's! My heart dropped with a thud.

"And it's still *you* that I want to fill that space," Joanne continued. "If you could give me a couple of 'think pieces' a month — you know, maybe start off with something about teen suicide, then tackle an issue like peer pressure or loneliness." Her cheeks had taken on bright red spots of enthusiasm. But I refused to listen one second longer.

Having been a witness to Brian's firing, I should have known better than to appeal to Mrs. Caprice, but I couldn't help myself. "Mrs. Caprice, a few weeks ago, Katie told me you took a readers' survey that proved more kids than ever are picking up the paper just because of my column," I said in a voice quavering with anger. "Don't you see that the circulation will go down if you drop it? The school district might even cut the newspaper budget."

Mrs. Caprice cleared her throat and smiled thinly. "Joanne has some excellent ideas for new regular features that should draw every bit as much interest as 'Lori's Listening' did."

I snorted, stood up, and headed for the door.

"Don't go," Joanne called. "If you don't like the idea of doing think pieces, I'll run down some of the new features, and you can have first dibs."

"No, thanks," I snapped.

"Oh, don't be so childish," Joanne said. "I really *do* like your writing. You have a very accessible style, very conversational. It would be a shame not to use you elsewhere on the paper. The sports editorship, for example, has just opened up — "

I went out the door and tried to slam it, which was impossible, since, like all school doors, it was on one of those air devices that force it to close quietly and gradually.

I wandered out to the parking lot in a daze of despair and disbelief. Where was Big Guy when I needed him? His car was nowhere to be seen. In fact, the entire student parking lot was nearly deserted. Glancing at my watch, I saw to my surprise that it was almost four. Not knowing about my meeting with Joanne, Big Guy must have given up waiting for me for our usual Thursday-afternoon tutoring session.

I trudged on home, labeling Joanne under my breath with every swear word I could think of: "Joanne, you _____; Joanne, you _____; Joanne, you _____."

It was no longer raining, but the streets had that damp, musty, depressing after-storm smell and the sky was gray and heavy, like my mood. I began to pass people puttering in their yards, and I kept my head down, not wanting to talk to anyone. Finally, I had to put a hand over my mouth to stifle a cry of pain. *What was I going to do without my column? I'd be a nobody — nothing more than just your basic average freshman like everybody else.*

Turning the corner onto my street, I felt a sudden flash of warmth. I looked up to see that the sun had broken through just one tiny corner of the muddy sky and was cascading down in golden columns to solely spotlight . . . Megan and Big Guy!

Once again, my heart sank. No, not just sank — it absolutely burst. My body froze on the sidewalk, but my eyes were riveted on the sight. It couldn't be . . . *it just couldn't be*.

But it was. Standing close together, they were leaning against Big Guy's Impala, which sparkled whitely in the rays of sunshine. It was parked at the curb between my house and the Marshes'.

Suddenly, my feet came unglued, and I was flying toward them. *Get there . . . get there . . . get there — before he falls under her spell.*

Despite the noisiness of my feet pounding the pavement, neither Big Guy nor Megan even glanced in my direction. Not even when I was standing right in front of them.

"Big Guy!" I shouted.

As if in slow motion, he forced his eyes away from Megan and turned to me, and for several seconds it seemed as if he didn't recognize me.

I glared at Megan, and she just laughed softly — a low, delighted laugh. Grabbing Big Guy's arm, I frantically pulled him toward my house. Like some sort of stunned rag doll, he allowed himself to be pulled, but he walked backward, his eyes never leaving Megan.

I dragged him through our front door and into the family room, glad to see that my mother wasn't home to witness this humiliation. He was acting like a lovesick zombie.

"Big Guy!" I said, shaking him. "What were you doing on my street? Why did you come here? I told you not to!"

Finally, he seemed to regain his senses. He shook himself like a dog. "I . . . I came because I had to talk to you," he said. "I came to tell you that I think it's best that we start dating other people — "

I howled with anger. "Liar! You came here for no such purpose. You came here because it was a tutoring day and you couldn't find me after school and you got worried about me."

He ducked his head, making me positive I was right.

"You didn't get this date-other-people idea until you happened to run into that Megan Marsh a few minutes ago!" I shouted.

He took a deep breath. "I came to tell you that I think it's best that we start dating other people. You've been so cool and distant and mysterious lately — I just don't feel close to you anymore. I just don't feel like a part of your life."

"But Big Guy, I — "

"You don't need me to tutor you anymore, either," he interrupted. "Barclay says you're doing B-level work."

"But that's only because you're helping me every other — "

"And anyway, I think your parents want us to break up, too," he continued, ignoring me. "I mean, I think the real reason they restricted you from dating is that they don't want you seeing so much of just one guy. They don't want you getting serious so young. Come on, Lori, admit that I'm right."

I slapped my forehead. "But you're not!" I launched into a long, impassioned, and rather pathetic plea about why we couldn't break up, why we were the perfect couple. But I knew it was useless. It was simply too late. The inevitable had happened.

Big Guy turned his back on me and went to stand at the window. I knew he was gazing longingly at the Marshes' house.

After a few minutes, he just strode out the front door without a word. I sank in a heap onto the floor exactly where he'd left me standing and just cried and cried. All in one day, I had lost my job, my boyfriend, and my social position.

My mother came looking for me for dinner a couple of hours later and found me still in that same position in the now pitch-dark room. Without a word, she gently led me away. Through the window, I could see that Big Guy's car was still parked outside, shining under the streetlight.

Chapter 13

The next few weeks were as bleak and desolate as any I can remember. When I didn't have to drag myself to school, I spent practically every minute hibernating in my bedroom with the shade pulled down. I couldn't bear even an accidental glimpse out that window. It would only confirm how much time *he* was spending at *her* house.

There were just two times I couldn't resist a peak behind the shade. The first was when Aunt Marsh and Amanda brought Bethanny home from the hospital. She was a thinner, ghostlier version of her already-pale former self, thanks to a severe bout of pneumonia complicated by some intestinal thing. My heart lurched when I saw how she clung to Amanda's arm for support.

The other time I allowed myself to look down

at the Marshes' house was when Captain and Mrs. Marsh came home from the airport by taxi. He was a tall, gaunt skeleton, smiling painfully and leaning on a cane. Though I'd never seen him before, it was obvious the man had been thoroughly ravaged by disease. Even though the book said only Bethanny would die, I wondered if the Marshes would soon be holding a double funeral.

A few days later, however, that possibility seemed unlikely. I was having breakfast in the kitchen with my dad when the Captain came over to introduce himself to our family. He looked tanner and heavier already, said he'd be playing golf daily starting Monday, and declared he felt more "chipper" every day.

Bethanny, however, was a different story. I could often hear her coughing violently in the Marshes' sunny garden, where she no doubt lay heavily blanketed on the chaise longue. Sometimes I would set down my book — I was rereading my entire collection of classics except for *that* one — and strain to hear if her cough was getting worse. Other times, I would clap my hands over my ears and sing "Boys Are Made of Greasy Grimy Gopher Guts" to drown out the pitiful hacking.

Rereading my old favorites helped to fill the time I used to devote to column matters. Still, because I was doing little more than flopping around on my bed to change reading positions hour after hour, I couldn't squelch the feeling of being totally lost and useless and at loose ends without "Lori's Listening." How in the world, I wondered, had I ever filled up 24 hours a day before I became a columnist?

Nor did the books allow me to escape the constant, terrible pain and jealousy of losing Big Guy, no matter how inevitable it had been. Or the helpless frustration of waiting for Bethanny to die. Why were the classics so full of people getting sick or getting married? Sometimes I just sat on the floor, hugged myself, and rocked back and forth for hours, completely consumed by misery.

To my surprise, on the second Friday after Black Thursday, two popular seniors invited me to their weekend parties.

"But haven't you heard?" I muttered to Dani McDade, head cheerleader. "My column's been cancelled."

"Yeah, I heard," she said. "But I want you to come anyway."

"But haven't you heard?" I muttered. "B.G. Grimes and I have broken up."

Dani heaved an exasperated sigh. "Yeah, I heard that, too. But I want you to come anyway."

My conversation with Jade Fontana about her party was almost identical.

These people wanted me for *myself*? Nah . . . I just couldn't believe it. That kind of discovery was limited to main characters in contemporary teen novels. My jaded little mind feverishly sorted through the possible *real* motives behind these invitations, and the best it could come up with was my brother, Kevin. Maybe these girls hoped that by staying in my favor they would somehow endear themselves to Mr. Wonderful (as he often referred to himself in the privacy of our own home).

But that theory really didn't hold up, not when I thought it through. Both Jade and Dani were already good friends of Kevin's, so they didn't need me to get close to him. Besides, each girl already had a boyfriend.

Once I ruled out ulterior motives, I began to feel a little better about myself. In fact, I even decided to go to Dani's party. Well, actually, that decision also required a little coaxing from Kerry *plus* the guarantee that she and Dieter would find a guy for me to go with, so I wouldn't have to tag along with them like some sort of chaperone.

But the evening turned out to be a total and complete disaster.

The worst part was that *he* was there with

her, to my utter shock. It had just never occurred to me that he would have the gall to bring her to one of *our* school's parties. But there they were, all cuddly on the couch in the center of Dani's living room. The only time he took his starry eyes off her was to make jealous, growling noises at guys who approached them in hopes of meeting "that gorgeous babe," as I overheard one guy refer to her.

Naturally, I was ready to leave the party three and a half minutes after we got there. I managed to convince my date, Kyle, Dieter's biology lab partner, that I must have a Big Mac *immediately*. I knew full well that the closest McDonald's was a mile and a half away and that we'd have to walk it, since we'd come in Dieter's car and Kyle didn't have a license. He didn't seem to mind leaving the party, having done nothing since we got there except get on his hands and knees to peer at Dani's father's stereo system from a variety of angles.

That should have tipped me off, for sure. It soon became clear that this guy couldn't utter *one word* that wasn't related to the subject of stereo components. I trudged along on the sidewalk beside him, yawning till my eyes watered as he mumbled a monologue full of Dolby and woofers and tweeters and other terms that were Greek to me plus a string of Japanese brand names: Sanyo-Sansui-Sony . . . snore.

He was so absorbed in his own discussion that when we finally got to McDonald's he accidentally ordered me a "Big DAT," which was evidently yet another sound system word. The guy at the counter, obviously a fellow stereo nerd, laughed like a hyena and called Kyle "bro."

A few minutes later, I told Kyle that the "Big DAT" I'd eaten had made me queasy and that I wanted to go home instead of back to the party. He walked me home, cheerfully continuing his stereo monologue. Mentally, I clapped my hands over my ears and sang "Boys Are Made of Greasy Grimy Gopher Guts" to drown him out.

There was one bright spot as the weeks of misery continued.

It happened on a Tuesday after school, when I was moping around in my darkened bedroom, as usual.

All of a sudden, someone began to rap on our front door with the brass knocker so hard and so insistently I was afraid the door would break down. My mother was out running errands, so I raced downstairs. It sounded like a real emergency.

I glanced through the peephole and there, to

my surprise, stood *Bethanny*. I threw the door open. Her cheeks were rosy, her hair was shiny . . . she looked better than I'd ever seen her.

Bethanny picked up the case that was sitting at her feet and shoved it into my stomach. "Here!" she shouted. "Tell your mother thanks! As for you, thanks for nothing!" I recognized the case as I grabbed it to keep it from falling. It was my mother's Smith-Corona typewriter.

Bethanny whirled around and started to stalk across our lawn.

I finally recovered my voice. "Bethanny? Wait! What's the matter?"

She whirled back around, eyes blazing. "I'll tell you what's the matter!" She marched back to our front porch, taking a piece of paper out of her jacket pocket and waving it at me. "I have a lot of schoolwork to catch up on, so I came over last night to see if you guys had a typewriter I could borrow," Bethanny shouted. She pointed at the typewriter in my arms. "Your mother found that for me in your garage . . . and when I got home, I found *this* inside it." Again, she waved the piece of paper, this time in front of my nose.

I snatched it from her and turned blood-red. It was a spare "summary slip" from the nurse's office . . . or at least it was one of the photocopies I'd made on which to type the bogus reports.

In vivid, four-letter terms, the tamest of which was "puke," Bethanny began to screech about what she thought of me for sabotaging her job in the nurse's office "for no other reason but malice!"

I just stood there, gaping at her, unable to believe that this was sweet little Bethanny. Suddenly, I saw Kerry crossing the street. She was no doubt coming over on one of her every other day "snap-out-of-it-Lori" missions. She stopped on the sidewalk, several feet away from us, and watched with her mouth hanging open. I was sure the whole neighborhood could hear Bethanny's diatribe.

Finally, Bethanny called me "vile, gutter-slinking slime" and stormed off across the lawn and through the hedge, vowing that "I will never, *ever* speak to you again, Lori Laigen!"

Thoughtfully, I stared after her a minute.

Kerry joined me on the porch. "Wow," she said, "if *Bethanny Marsh* considers you gutter-slinking slime . . . well, that about puts you on a par with guys like Hitler and Jack the Ripper."

I turned to her. "She discovered that I was the one responsible for her being fired from the nurse's office."

"Oh, was that it? I couldn't really make out *what* she was getting at in between all those nath-ty words."

Suddenly, I threw my head back and laughed joyfully, then danced around in a circle.

Kerry shook me. "Are you going crackers, girl? I know you don't much care what she thinks, but being screeched at is a rather sobering experience for most people."

"How can I be anything but happy and relieved, Kerry?" I sang. "Don't you see? Bethanny isn't going to die. I just realized it."

Kerry followed me into the house, and we sat down on the couch in the family room. "Now what makes you say that?" she asked. "I thought you were more convinced than ever that the Marsh girls and the March girls share the same fates. Especially since you-know-who started going with you-know-who."

Her words sparked a twinge of pain, but I ignored it. "Well, I'm still convinced that what we've got going is some sort of *Twilight Zone* phenomenon," I said slowly. "Through some weird twist in history or a black hole in time or whatever, we're seeing *Little Women* being played out in real life."

I got up and began pacing. "But obviously, technology is intervening and updating at least *some* of the story for the late twentieth century," I continued. "Take penicillin, for example, which they didn't have in Louisa May Alcott's days. It's cured *this* Beth."

Kerry looked at me skeptically.

"Oh, come on, Ker, you saw her!" I said. "She's never looked better! And all that shrieking she did — my, my! Such out-of-character rage. Believe me, the Beth in the book never even raises her voice, let alone shouts obscenities."

Kerry snickered.

I smiled. "To me, that's just more evidence that she's completely recovered. I tell you, I'm convinced that *that* Marsh girl, at least, is not going to share the fate of her fictional counterpart."

Kerry jumped up and took my hands. "But then, don't you see? If the part about Bethanny dying isn't going to come true why can't there be that same possibility about Megan marrying Big Guy?"

I sighed. "Because, unfortunately, nothing has yet been invented to cure Big Guy of the way he feels about Megan. I'm afraid all we can do is let the rest of the story play out, as written, to the last page."

Chapter 14

That night, I sat struggling over an English composition that was due the next day. I had chosen "What I *Won't* Do On My Summer Vacation" from Ms. Toffler's list of topics. But thanks to the discussion I'd had with Kerry, my mind kept veering off onto the subject of fate and whether it was real and whether if could be changed. By nine-thirty, I had managed to write only one really stupid sentence on the summer vacation topic. That's when I decided to just trash it and go with what was on my mind. After all, Ms. Toffler didn't force us to pick one of her topics.

"Fate: Fact or Fiction?" I wrote on the top of a clean sheet of paper, and then the words just poured out of me.

Sometimes I believe in fate so strongly that I just stop whatever I'm doing and lie down on my bed, feeling a curious mixture of both peace and frustration. I think, if there is such a thing as fate, it has already been determined that, say, I'm going to go to Stanford and then will become an architect. So why should I worry about something like finishing a composition for my English class? Why not just go downstairs and watch TV and show up in English empty-handed? After all, nothing I do will change my fate; nothing I do will change the fact that I've been dealt an eventual Stanford degree and an architectural practice.

At other times, I'm sure that fate is just a word invented by fortune-tellers to increase business. I usually feel that way whenever I hear about a kid dying in a fire or a crash. Surely if there were such a thing as fate, it couldn't be both so wonderful as to ensure that one person grows up beautiful and becomes a movie star and also so cruel as to decide that some innocent little kid has to die at age five.

It's because I don't know whether we determine our own destinies or whether

*we are ruled by fate that I go on trying
and wondering and hoping and doing my
best . . . just to play it safe either way.*

I went on in this same vein for another page
and a half. Then I read it back, adding commas.
It was good! When I turned the light out at
eleven, I felt more satisfied with myself than
I had in weeks, maybe even years.

That weekend, I had dates for both Friday
and Saturday nights.

On Friday, I went out with Dalton Feeney,
one of Dieter's swim team pals. Despite his
name, he was a very good-looking blond, and
I had high hopes that this might turn into something long-term.

Like practically everybody else at school, we
went to the Corvette Café, which had adver-
tised a special high school show that night. A
disc jockey from my favorite radio station was
to broadcast live, and there was also a stand-
up comedian and a couple of local garage bands
on the menu.

When we got there, Dalton deposited me
at the table next to Kerry and Dieter's, asked
me to order him a hamburger with nothing
on it, and promptly took off for the men's
room.

I ordered for us. Twenty minutes passed. The food came. Still no sign of Dalton. I nibbled on a cold french fry. Sue Ann, one of those older waitresses who calls everyone "hon," came by to refill my water glass. She glanced at Dalton's untouched hamburger, and I realized she'd never seen him.

"Listen, hon, don't feel too bad," she said, whisking Dalton's plate away. "Every gal gets stood up now and again."

"But I haven't been stood up," I bleated. "He's *here*. He's just in the bathroom."

She clicked her tongue sympathetically and took off. I could tell she didn't believe me.

I reached over the back of my booth and poked Dieter. "Go see what his problem is!" I hissed.

Dieter came back a few minutes later, shaking his head. "Dalton's not feeling so hot. He doesn't look so hot, either. Kind of green."

"Well, he can look kind of green out here, can't he?" I said.

"He's afraid the smell of food will make him lose it," Dieter said. "Just give him a few minutes, will ya? Maybe this thing'll pass."

I gave him a whole hour. I know how lonely and forlorn I must have looked to people passing that table. Sue Ann — that sadist — had by then whisked away every sign that I was there with a date, even the phantom Dalton's water glass. Finally, Kerry and Dieter abandoned their table and joined me at mine out of sympathy.

"I was even starting to wish that I was here with *Kyle*, talking woofers and tweeters," I muttered to Kerry. "He, at least, was a living, breathing body."

Kerry sighed. "Lori's Losers."

I just glared at her.

"Which reminds me of Megan's Morons," she said. "Which reminds me that you-know-who and you-know-who aren't here."

Of course I knew that. I'd had my eye on the door practically since we'd walked in, but Big Guy and Megan never showed. What a relief! I shuddered to think of him getting a look at me sitting prim and red-faced in lone splendor at my table. Miss Desirable.

Two hours gone. The show started.

Then three hours. The show ended. Dieter made one final trip to the bathroom and back. "Guess I'll be taking you home, Lori," he said with a sheepish shrug. "Dalton doesn't feel he can drive."

At that point, I'd just had it. "Besides never again setting me up with one of your pals, Dieter, you can do me one final favor," I snapped. "Go back in there and give this to

Dalton." I handed him the bill Sue Ann had brought. Then I snatched it back. Sue Ann had written "Thanks much, hon" across the bottom in big curlicue letters. I added "For your *scintillating* company," returned the bill to Dieter, and gave him a shove toward the men's room.

On Saturday night, I went out with Gary Spevak, a newer friend of my brother, whom I'd met recently in our very own family room. He was right on the borderline between too skinny and slim, but he was nice and tall, had a handsome face, and laughed a lot.

Gary wanted to go to a party at Todd Killigrew's house, a party to which Todd had also invited me. Though I had avoided parties since Dani's — unable to bear the thought of seeing Big Guy with Megan again — I eventually let Gary talk me into this one. I didn't tell him why I was so reluctant to go, but I think he suspected. He promised that if I didn't like the party we would leave any time I wanted to, no matter how early, and go to a movie. No questions asked.

It turned out we didn't leave the party early. Like the night before at the Corvette, Big Guy and Megan never showed. He wants to be alone with her, I thought sadly. But I managed to have a pretty good time anyway. True to his word, about every half hour or so — not often enough to be irritating — Gary asked if I wanted to leave.

That was the thing about him — he was really a nice guy. And he did everything right: chatted with my dad for a few minutes when he picked me up, complimented me on my new leather skirt, asked me questions about myself when we were alone, and stuck with me at Todd's party.

Somehow, though, he just seemed sort of lackluster compared to Big Guy. Dry toast. Vanilla ice cream. Creamed corn. Actually — I looked around at the other guys at the party a few times — *all* guys seemed that way.

And that's why, even though it'd been the nicest evening I'd spent in a long time, I still cried myself to sleep that night, as usual. Was I doomed to go through life rejecting every guy I met because no one could compare to *him*?

On Monday, in Spanish, a monitor brought me a note from Mrs. Caprice. She asked me to meet her and Joanne in the newspaper office right after school. I figured they were going to take another stab at forcing the sports editorship on me.

To my surprise, the two of them stood up and beamed at me as I came through the door.

"We love it!" Joanne said.

"And we're going to run it, dear," Mrs. Caprice said, handing me a piece of paper.

I glanced at it as I sat down. It was a photocopy of my essay on fate. "But how did you get — ?"

"Ms. Toffler was so impressed with it that she sent it over to be considered for the newspaper," Mrs. Caprice explained. "Some of the English teachers do that, you know."

I gave her a goofy smile. "Guess that means I got an A on the thing."

Joanne was rubbing her hands together. "Didn't I tell you she'd be a whiz at think pieces?" she said to Mrs. Caprice. Joanne turned to me. "How can I convince you to submit more essays like this one directly to me on a regular basis?"

That's when I was struck by inspiration — negotiation! "I'd love to," I said sweetly, "provided you also let me do 'Lori's Listening' again." Oh, how I still missed having my finger on the pulse of the school social scene!

Joanne narrowed her eyes. "No."

"Okay, then, a *shortened* version of 'Lori's Listening,' " I offered.

"No."

Suddenly, I was determined that *this* Marsh

girl, at least, wasn't going to get *everything* she wanted. "That's my price," I said. "Take it or leave it."

"Then we have nothing more to talk about," Joanne said. She turned her back to me and busied herself with a pile of papers on the table.

I rose with exquisite grace and dignity. "You have my permission to print this one," I said haughtily, handing my essay back to Mrs. Caprice and pretending that Joanne did not exist. "But don't expect any more where this one came from." Nose in the air, I swept from the room.

Chapter 15

Joanne's "we have nothing more to talk about" were the last words ever spoken to me by any of the Marsh sisters. Because of those vague Kahlil Gibran quotes, I guess, Amanda continued to avoid me as if I were the neighborhood witch lady. Bethanny kept her vow to never speak to me again because of her typewriter discovery. And Megan knew better than to even come close.

Actually, if you can count an anonymous note I found in my locker one day, Bethanny, at least, did speak to me one last time. The note praised me for my "Fate" essay, which had run on the front page of the school newspaper that day. The handwriting was really inconsistent — some of the letters slanted left, some slanted right; some "i's" were dotted, others were given lightning bolts. In short, it looked like someone with neat handwriting had tried to make her handwriting look messy. The real tip-off, however, was the apology at the bottom of the note: "I am so sorry this is such a mess!"

Bethanny — or at least I was 98 percent sure it was Bethanny — wasn't the only person to compliment me on that essay. Others came up to me in the next few days to tell me the thing had "really made me think," or "was exactly how I feel," or that it "made me kind of uncomfortable" (which I considered a compliment).

In the end, I probably got slightly less feedback on the essay than I used to get after a typical "Lori's Listening" column. But somehow, the compliments about "Fate" meant 1000 times more to me. After all, they were praising something that came entirely from my head, not from the big mouths of others. And I didn't have to be so jaded as to wonder if people were just saying nice things in hopes of rating a good mention in my next column.

The day my essay ran in the paper, a gorgeous, summer-is-coming day, was the first in a long time that I pulled the shade up in my bedroom when I got home from school. No, I hadn't gotten over the Big Guy–Megan situation. But I hadn't heard the humph-humph-

humph of Big Guy's old gas hog V–8 engine on our street for days.

I was pretty sure the reason for this was that his mom was making him work in her antique store. I had just happened to see his car parked in front of it on three separate afternoons. Obviously, his mom's regular clerk had quit or was on vacation. I managed to walk sedately past the shop on those three afternoons, head and eyes frozen straight ahead, certain that if I glanced in the window, I would see Megan in there, too.

I could just picture them together in the shop, eyes and arms entwined, probably on that cherry-wood love seat Mrs. Grimes could never sell because she wanted too much for it. In fact, the image of Big Guy and Megan on that love seat was so crystal-clear and unchanging that it haunted my dreams every night for a week, and I started to believe that I really had caught a glimpse of them that way. All of the jealousy I thought I'd finally gotten under control — by constantly reminding myself that "what happened was inevitable" — came crashing back over me like storm waves, green and seething. I was suddenly sure Megan and Big Guy were on the verge of an ecstatic engagement announcement, the first step in their happily-ever-after.

So that's what I figured he'd come to tell me the Saturday morning I heard a humph-humph-humph in *our* driveway. Wasn't that the gentlemanly thing to do? Break the news first to the girl he'd dumped for the girl of his dreams?

I was sitting at the kitchen table eating Cheerios. My mother was rinsing dishes at the sink.

"It's B.G. Grimes," she said, peering through the Levelor blinds on the kitchen window. "Coming *here*. Did you guys make up?"

"No." I pretended to be deeply engrossed in the morning paper.

My mom went to the door and came back with him, then graciously disappeared.

He stood in front of me, eyes on the floor, red-faced.

"Excuse me, but you seem to have the wrong house," I said frostily. "Megan Marsh lives next door." I jerked a thumb in that direction.

His eyes shot up and met mine. "But I'm not seeing Megan anymore. I thought you knew that."

I hid my surprise and packed my voice with more ice. "Now how would I know that? Perhaps *you* didn't know that I am no longer the recipient of every unimportant tidbit of information circulating at school."

He shook his head. "No, I meant I thought one of the Marsh girls would have told you."

"I haven't been in communication with any of the Marsh girls for some weeks now." I was trying so hard to sound mature but it was instead coming out *snooty* — a fake British accent was creeping in. I looked down, remembered I was eating a very sophisticated bowl of Cheerios, and felt ridiculous.

He didn't seem to notice. "Well, I haven't talked to any of the Marsh girls in weeks, either," he said. "Including Megan."

Uninvited, he pulled out a chair and sat down across from me. "Not that I ever did much talking with her when we *were* going out. She doesn't have much to say. Unless it's about clothes or other guys she's dated."

A thrill of satisfaction shot through me, but I pretended to concentrate on eating my cereal.

"Megan is the only person I've ever met who is both a couch potato *and* a certified airhead," Big Guy continued. "I've learned you can only spend a finite amount of time just looking at someone before you go out of your mind with boredom." He rolled his eyes.

I hardened my heart. "Look, why did you come here? Why are you telling me this? Are you looking for advice? Approval? Do I look like Ann Landers?"

He reached across the table and grabbed my hand. I tried to pull away, but his hand was like a vise. "I came to say how sorry I am that what happened happened. And that I'm sorry for the way I handled it. But most of all that I want you to give me another chance."

I was melting, melting. His turquoise eyes held mine as tightly as his hand gripped my fingers.

"I miss you so much — the days are so long without you," he said in a rush. "I've even been working in my mom's store after school every day just to kill time. Lori, it took me two weeks to get up the courage to come and talk to you."

A little voice started whispering in my ear: "Forgive him, already. Take him back. He couldn't help falling for Megan, just like Bethanny was doomed to get sick. It was out of their hands." The little voice hummed the theme song from the *Twilight Zone*.

"Shut up," I said to it.

"What?" Big Guy asked.

"Not you," I said.

He stared at me for a minute, puzzled, then let go of my hand. "I was positive you'd slam the door in my face the minute you saw me," he said, "but you know what finally made me decide to try to see you anyway? That terrific essay you wrote. Especially the one part where you said that you keep on trying, keep on hoping, keep on doing your best because you don't know whether your future is already set in stone or not. If mine is, I just know you're in it. But if it isn't, then I have to do everything in my power to make sure you're going to be there, because a future without you sounds terrible. It sounds unbearable."

Abruptly I got up and went to the sink to dump the excess Cheerios. The connection he was trying to make between my essay and our relationship seemed a little shaky. And the self-righteous tone of voice and swooping gestures he had used reminded me so much of our minister giving a sermon that I had to bite back a laugh. But I was truly touched by his effort. More than that, it was at that minute in that sun-splashed kitchen on that May morning that I realized that I loved him and that to not give him another chance would be the worst mistake of my life.

I tried to turn around and tell him so, but for some reason I just couldn't. Then I glanced out the window over the sink. Piling into the family van, laden with wicker picnic baskets, were Captain and Mrs. Marsh, the four laughing, chattering Marsh sisters . . . and a new, good-looking guy who was trailing after Megan in a daze. Immediately, I felt a surge of remembered jealousy and anger. And that's when I understood what was holding me back from giving Big Guy another chance. I decided to just lay it on the line.

I rinsed my bowl and spoon, put them in the dishwasher, and turned around to face him. His eyes were wide and bright with hope.

"I just don't know if our getting back together again would work out," I said slowly. "Because every time I see Megan, I'll remember — and it'll hurt. Or it'll make me mad at you all over again."

He let out his breath in a gust of relief. "Is that all? Well, then, I have news for you. You won't be living next door to the Marshes very much longer."

I raised an eyebrow skeptically.

"It's true," he said. "Yesterday in the library, I overheard Joanne telling another girl that Captain Marsh is retiring from the Navy this summer. The whole family is moving to a ranch in Escondido. They're going to open a — "

"Boys' school?" I interrupted with a groan.

"Yeah. For problem kids. Runaways and so forth. How did you know? I thought you weren't speaking to any of them."

I went to his chair, bent over, and hugged him from behind. "Listen, Big Guy," I said, "I know that family like a book."

About the Author

Jacqueline Shannon, the second of four sisters, grew up in Southern California. After graduating from college with a degree in journalism, she held various jobs as a photojournalist, magazine editor, and TV reporter. She is now a full-time writer of novels and magazine pieces and lives in San Diego with her husband, Stephen, and their new baby, Madeline. Her articles and short stories have appeared frequently in such magazines as *Seventeen*, *Teen*, and *YM*. *Big Guy, Little Women* is her fifth novel.

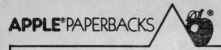

The Girls of Canby Hall®

by Emily Chase

School pressures! Boy trouble! Roommate rivalry! The girls of Canby Hall are learning about life and love now that they've left home to live in a private boarding school.

☐ 41212-4	#1	Roommates	$2.50
☐ 42048-8	#2	Our Roommate Is Missing	$2.50
☐ 40080-0	#3	You're No Friend of Mine	$2.25
☐ 41417-8	#4	Keeping Secrets	$2.50
☐ 40082-7	#5	Summer Blues	$2.25
☐ 40083-5	#6	Best Friends Forever	$2.25
☐ 41277-9	#19	One Boy Too Many	$2.50
☐ 40392-3	#20	Friends Times Three	$2.25
☐ 40657-4	#21	Party Time!	$2.50
☐ 40711-2	#22	Troublemaker	$2.50
☐ 40833-X	#23	But She's So Cute	$2.50
☐ 41055-5	#24	Princess Who?	$2.50
☐ 41090-3	#25	The Ghost of Canby Hall	$2.50
☐ 41371-6	#26	Help Wanted!	$2.50
☐ 41390-2	#27	The Roommate and the Cowboy	$2.50
☐ 41516-6	#28	Happy Birthday Jane	$2.50
☐ 41671-5	#29	A Roommate Returns	$2.50
☐ 41672-3	#30	Surprise!	$2.50
☐ 41673-1	#31	Here Comes the Bridesmaid	$2.50
☐ 42149-2	#32	Who Has a Crush on Andy?	$2.50

Complete series available wherever you buy books.

Scholastic Inc.
P.O. Box 7502, 2932 East McCarty Street, Jefferson City, MO 65102

Please send me the books I have checked above. I am enclosing $_____ (please add $1.00 to cover shipping and handling). Send check or money order— no cash or C.O.D.'s please.

Name_____

Address_____

City_____State/Zip_____
Please allow four to six weeks for delivery. Offer good in U.S.A. only. Sorry, mail order not available to residents of Canada. Prices subject to change.   CAN888